Watch The World End Publications

# The Faulty Process Of Electing A Senior Class President

Chris Dietzel

ISBN-10: 0692809627
ISBN-13: 978-0692809624

Cover design and typography: Everpage Designs
Editor: D.L. Mackenzie
Author photo: Jodie McFadden
More information on the author: www.ChrisDietzel.com

# ALSO BY CHRIS DIETZEL

# THE FAULTY PROCESS OF ELECTING A SENIOR CLASS PRESIDENT

Watch The World End Publications

# CONTENTS

FALL SEMESTER

# 1

On that first day of school, three students intended to become the next senior class president.

Shelly McMarton was on a mission. Her royal blue Tesla was ahead of every other sleek and expensive vehicle in the line forming at the entrance to United Exceptionalism. As soon as she parked, she got out and went directly toward the main building.

Chet Booth was three cars behind Shelly, driving his black Mercedes-Benz coupe with tinted windows. Chet's face was covered with acne scars even though no one had seen him go through the phase where he actually had pimples. His fingertips tapped on the steering wheel to match the beat of an old folk song that played from twelve strategically placed speakers all around him. The volume was at a level low enough to guarantee he would not suffer hearing loss.

The third student interested in becoming United Exceptionalism's next senior class president wasn't in the line of cars waiting to get an early start to the new school year. Reginald Cript was still sound asleep. Instead of meeting with his faculty advisor, as Shelly and Chet were going to do, Reginald thought that all he had to do was wake up, arrive to class, and declare he was going to make the academy better.

\*\*\*

The United Exceptionalism Academy for Boys and Girls had earned a reputation for excellence that was unmatched. All parents dreamed of their children attending the academy. Any student who cared about his or her future knew that getting into the school was the first step to a life of opportunity and privilege few others could access.

The academy ranked first in quality of education and resources for its students. It was first in the number of graduates who went on to attend Ivy League colleges. It even offered the luxury of international summer field trips.

Besides having the best teachers and finest facilities, the academy was acclaimed for preparing its students in ways that other schools did not. One method it did this was by allowing its student government to carry out most of the functions ordinarily performed by the school's administration. As a result, when the boys and girls at United Exceptionalism elected their senior class president, they weren't simply selecting someone to choose a prom theme or organize a car wash; they were selecting someone who would set the course for the academy and make decisions that would impact the institution for the next school year and beyond. At other schools, this would have been considered reckless. But at United Exceptionalism it was just another way to prepare its students for the real world.

The academy did not simply teach its youth. It created leaders.

\*\*\*

Crossing the parking lot, Shelly frowned at the automatic beep of her car's security system, which was louder than she preferred. Before reaching the double doors of the academy, she straightened her pink pantsuit, ready to begin her junior year and her quest for senior class president.

She knew the other kids laughed at the clothes she wore but it didn't matter to her. Other girls wore skirts of varying lengths. Some wore jeans or shorts with button-up shirts, sweaters, or blouses. (Most private schools required the students to wear uniforms but one of United Exceptionalism's previous senior class presidents had decided to do away with them.) Other than Shelly, none of the other girls would dare be seen in a pantsuit combination. It was all Shelly wore, though. She had one in every color. Starburst Yellow. Grandstand Green. Polite Plum.

She wore pantsuits for two reasons. The first was that there was no better way for someone to look professional than to wear a suit. It was true of men and damn if it wasn't true for women of all ages as well. The other reason she wore them was because of her oddly shaped body. Her legs were the opposite of a tall drink of water. Her wide waist made her shoulders seem peculiarly narrow. Knowing how brutal children could be over the tiniest of imperfections, she had taken matters into her own hands.

When she became their next leader, the kids would have to respect her.

***

It was nice to be the starting quarterback of the varsity football team, but very few of the school's athletes went on to achieve the same level of success as its student politicians. No one could remember the names of prom kings and queens of years past. The opposite was true of each senior class president. Most of them went on to become prominent and influential members of society. Nearly two hundred boys and girls had been elected senior president over the academy's long history and the majority had gone on to become CEOs, billionaires, professional politicians, or all three.

The role was so important that the election process for senior class president started at the beginning of the students' junior year. Starting in September and going through the entire fall, winter, and spring semesters, students vying for the office fought among themselves for the opportunity to lead the academy the following year. At the end of the spring semester, the election was held and the next senior class president was chosen.

***

To Shelly's side, sprinklers watered the academy's eighteen-hole golf course to maintain its brilliant shade of green. Although she couldn't see them from where she was, the two Olympic-size swimming pools were also in that direction. She entered the building without greeting any of the students who had pulled into the lot after her. Nor did she say hello or even smile at the janitor who was finishing mopping up the floors. Not even the old man liked her, she guessed. No one liked her. That was fine. She didn't like them either.

# 2

Within the United Exceptionalism Academy for Boys and Girls, two prevailing factions of students and alumni had formed over the years. One prided itself on cherishing the morals and principles that had gone into founding the academy. These people called themselves Traditionalists, and they sought to keep the mission of the school simple: provide the same services that had first been offered by the institution. The other group was always looking to make improvements to the academy. These people called themselves Reformists, and they sought to ensure the school they loved could adapt with the times.

As the decades went by, as technology and innovation created new ways the school could be run, there were frequent clashes over whether United Exceptionalism would remain exactly as it had been or if it would adapt with a changing world. Most times, compromise was achieved and the two sides got along. Other times, they didn't.

Over the years, the children of Traditionalists tended to become Traditionalists as well, just as the children of Reformists tended to adopt their parents' beliefs. With each decade, the lines between the Traditionalists and the Reformists became more distinct.

When it had first been suggested that each classroom be provided with a complement of computers, the Traditionalists were aghast. "No child needs to be surrounded by technology. We learned with pencils and paper and look how we turned out."

The Reformists saw an opportunity to outdo every other institution of learning. "If other schools are switching to computers with their limited budgets, just think about the types of computers we could afford."

Of course, it wasn't the principal or school administrator who ultimately made that decision. It was the senior class president.

***

Shelly's faculty advisor was a man who taught both the Microeconomics and Macroeconomics classes. As it happened, he had also been the faculty member assigned to every other successful Reformist candidate over the last ten years.

"Hello, Mr. Podulski," she said, giving a polite knock as she walked into his classroom.

The Economics teacher looked up from the first

day's lesson plan and nodded. "Shelly."

"We have a lot of work to do."

Mr. Podulski put aside his papers. "Indeed, we do."

"Well, let's get started."

The first bell hadn't even rung yet.

\*\*\*

Throughout the summer, the message to the Reformist parents had been clear: there would be no other challenger to Shelly in the first round of voting. She was their best shot at prevailing over the Traditionalists in the second round, so alumni and parents pressured the other children with aspirations of running for senior class president to find alternate ways of spending their time. Beth Warren, a popular girl who had gone to space camp at age seven, received her first patent at age nine, and won children's Jeopardy a year later, was told in no uncertain terms that she shouldn't run unless she wanted her teachers to find reasons to keep giving her detention. The few other interested students, the ones foolish enough to think they stood a chance against Shelly, were also threatened. All of them eventually got the message and watched from the sidelines for the inevitable winner to become the next senior class president.

\*\*\*

Things were nowhere near as cut and dried for the Traditionalists. Only two years earlier, Jorge M. Shrub, then senior class president, had been a complete disaster. The school was still reeling from the problems it had inherited under Shrub's tenure and it would continue to do so for many more years to come.

The problem started when a janitor working at the academy was badly beaten one morning and a fire set. This happened prior to any other faculty or students arriving. Poor old Mr. Glover was taken to the hospital, and while he did eventually recover, he had to walk with the assistance of a cane. The fire that had started at the side door where Mr. Glover was attacked destroyed much of one exterior wall and damaged a classroom. It was an attack the likes of which United Exceptionalism had never seen before. No one knew how to react. The police investigated but they were of little help.

"Whoever did it managed to avoid being caught on any of the security cameras," one cop said.

"They must have really hated that janitor," another said.

Shrub didn't need definitive proof of who had caused the attack. He went into immediate action. Iroquois Regional High School was on the other side of town. It was known for having a significant number of lower class students, kids who could barely afford meals and clothes and would never be admitted to an institution like United Exceptionalism. That was why Shrub said they had carried out the attack. It was because they resented what United Exceptionalism stood for.

All it took was Shrub hearing that Mr. Glover had a relative who attended Iroquois Regional High School for the senior class president to become convinced he was right. He wasn't sure of the specifics, but that didn't matter. What mattered was that United Exceptionalism would show everyone that it wasn't to be messed with.

After school the next day, Shrub sent the entire varsity football team to Iroquois Regional High School. The linebackers broke windows while the offensive and defensive linemen beat up every student they came across. The punter kicked over trashcans. The quarterback threw stones through car windows. The property damage was extensive, and a large portion of the high school's student body was injured. Almost every single part of the building was damaged in one way or another.

There was no telling what Shrub had been thinking when he ordered the attack, because any amount of forethought would have told him that the damage caused by United Exceptionalism's students would have to be paid out of the academy's own budget. He was lucky the police never arrested him for ordering it. Some of the football players weren't as fortunate.

The problems didn't stop there, however. A month later, a storm came through and part of the Chemistry lab's ceiling was damaged by water. Rather than removing the standing water and fixing the leak, Shrub ignored it. Predictably, the damage spread as more water made its way through the sub-roofing. The next time it rained, two adjacent classrooms also had water leaking from the ceiling.

When the roofing company was finally called, the contractor said the damage was extensive and would require replacing over four thousand square feet of the roof. "You know," he said, "it wouldn't have been so bad if you had called us out earlier."

It didn't make things look any better that the company that was hired to come in and fix the damage belonged to the father of one of Shrub's friends.

A month later, having learned nothing from the Iroquois High misadventure, Shrub sent the football team to destroy another high school and beat up their students. This time, the reasoning was that the students there might have been in cahoots with the troublemakers at Iroquois Regional High School.

Of course, it wasn't until Shrub graduated and was no longer senior class president that the police finally determined what had happened to poor old Mr. Glover. It hadn't been some kind of coordinated attack by kids who went to Iroquois. It had been a random drunk who avoided detection by dumb luck rather than strategic planning. He had been driving home from a nearby bar when he saw Mr. Glover outside during a smoke break, realized the man was alone, and decided to rob him. It was Mr. Glover's own cigarette that had started the fire. The cancer stick had fallen on the ground and ignited newly sprayed pesticides around the perimeter of the building, fueling the flames.

It would take years for the damage at Iroquois Regional High School to be forgotten. The money United Exceptionalism had to pay to fix the repairs had caused other programs at the academy to be cut back. The football team had gotten arrested for nothing. United Exceptionalism hadn't just suffered during Shrub's year as senior class president; some said it had barely survived.

\*\*\*

Because of that fiasco, the Traditionalists were adamant that they would never allow someone like Shrub to be their senior class president again. Over the summer, several students expressed interest in representing the Traditionalists as the senior class president candidate. The problem was they were all students who were groomed in the same manner as Shrub, meaning they were Traditionalist through and through or else had a parent who was an outspoken Traditionalist.

As a result, no matter how much their parents told them to consider the conventional options, the children refused to support anyone who had backed Shrub. Normally, this would have been seen as progress. Unfortunately for the Traditionalists, the only two students left were Reginald Cript and Chet Booth.

\*\*\*

Reginald Cript was the son of one of the richest men in the country. Everyone who sent their child to United Exceptionalism was quite wealthy, but Cript's father surpassed all of them. With little parental oversight and with an unlimited sense of entitlement, Cript became a teenage monster.

He gained notoriety throughout the school for being cruel to girls, a bully to any smaller boys, and vindictive to teachers who dared give him poor grades—even if they were deserved. Cript called one girl, a brunette who was only slightly overweight, a pig every chance he got. He also told her she should eat out of a trough and he made *oink* noises near her because he said it was how she should communicate. He ridiculed the captain of the cheerleading squad as a ditz who dated too many boys. Oddly enough, Cript thought he was charming her somehow. In some twisted triumph of teenage reverse psychology, he convinced her to go out on a date with him. She accepted on the condition he would stop making fun of her. When she got back to school the following Monday, everyone had heard a rumor that Cript had bedded another girl at the academy even though she insisted they hadn't even kissed.

Another of Cript's talents was that he knew how to get under people's skin and goad them into fights. However, when anyone challenged him physically, he threatened to have his dad's lawyers sue them. One day, all throughout class, Cript told the boy in front of him that he stank like shit. After being told this a dozen times, the boy, who had never stood up to anyone, got out of his chair and walked two desks over to where Cript sat laughing.

"Say that one more time," the boy demanded, a fist clenched, ready to strike.

Cript, seeing that the kid meant it, stopped smiling and said, "If you even touch me once, I'll have my dad's lawyers take your dad for everything he's worth. Do it. I dare you to do it. I'll sue you so hard you won't even have shit to call your own. Your parents will have to sell their crappy house."

Cript got by in the academy by having other people do his work for him. Other kids couldn't take his tests, though, and so those he failed. He was rumored to drop out of classes in order to prevent receiving a failing grade.

And yet, no one could deny that there was something irresistible about him, in the same way that no high school student could look away from a fistfight or a couple breaking up in the middle of the hallway. He was a bad action movie that people paid to see even though they knew the script was terrible. He was a cheap meal bought off a street corner even though it would make whoever ate it sick.

*** 

The other option was somehow just as bad. Chet Booth was routinely seen with snot hanging out of his nose. Every part of his face looked as though it were trying not to fall off a cliff. He had a goofy smile that remained on his face even when other kids viciously mocked him.

To Booth's credit, he refused to acknowledge anyone didn't like him. Even when the other students ridiculed him right to his face, Booth would laugh as if they were joking about someone else and he was joining them in the fun. It didn't often work in cutting short the mockery, but Booth never let it be seen that the mean words or the laughter bothered him.

Booth was detested for a lot of reasons. One was how much he refused to help others. Any time the teacher broke the class into groups, Booth would raise his hand and request to be allowed to work by himself. When the students were given a chance to choose which movie to watch in class or which speaker would be brought in for a guest lecture, regardless of whether every other student agreed on a selection, Booth would raise his hand and suggest a different option and then stir controversy until the event was ruined. The few times his obstruction was overruled, he refused to stay in class while the other

13

students watched the movie or listened to the guest speaker.

***

Chet Booth only accepted a faculty advisor after being assured the teacher was a man who shared all of Chet's characteristics. That is to say, Booth's advisor, a man of seventy years, divorced many times, was bitter, grumpy, and disliked by the rest of the faculty. A complete outcast.

On the other hand, Reginald Cript didn't even realize he was entitled to a faculty advisor. He simply walked into school that first day of his junior year and announced that he would be the senior class president. He said he would be the best one ever and that the girls had better line up early if they wanted a chance at dating him before his schedule became too busy.

These were the two Traditionalists who would vie for the chance to challenge Shelly McMarton. Needless to say, not many Traditionalist alumni were holding out hope that either boy might actually beat McMarton and become senior class president.

# 3

"I expect you know how this will go," Mr. Podulski said, tilting his head down so he could see Shelly over his reading glasses. "But I'm going to explain it to you anyway so there's no confusion and we get off on the right foot."

School wasn't scheduled to start for another hour. The academy's hallways were mostly quiet. Rather than sit at his own chair, Podulski walked over to the desk next to where Shelly was seated.

Mr. Podulski continued, "I'm here to help you become the next senior class president. To do that, I need you to be honest with me at all times."

"Okay."

The girl's response had been immediate, no hesitation.

Mr. Podulski took in a long breath, then exhaled. "Don't say 'okay'"—his voice rose to mimic hers—"unless you mean it. I'm going to be honest with you, sometimes brutally so, and you'll dislike me for it. I need you to be the same way for me. I'll start the honesty between us by stating what you probably already know: you have a reputation throughout the school for being dishonest and wholly untrustworthy. So you'll have to forgive me, but when I hear you say 'okay'"—he again adopted a mocking, high-pitched voice—"I don't quite believe you yet."

Shelly's eyes widened and her nostrils flared. She didn't say anything, though. Those who knew her had grown to fear this expression of hers. Not because they dreaded losing her friendship—she didn't have any friends to lose—but because they knew she held grudges. It was rumored that Shelly kept a little black book in her bedroom. The pages were supposedly filled with the names of people who had wronged her in one way or another and whom she would undoubtedly get payback on eventually. There was no way to know for sure if the little black book actually existed. No other students had been in Shelly's bedroom because no one wanted anything to do with her. And yet the rumor of the little black book persisted, mostly because Shelly herself whispered about its existence as a way to scare other children into abiding by her wishes or, at the very minimum, just leaving her alone.

"Spare me, Ms. McMarton. I'm here to help you and I'm your best shot at becoming senior class president.

I'm probably going to say much worse things to you over the next year so you'll have to get used to it. Do you understand?"

Shelly's lower lip trembled. The frequency of her blinking increased. It was impossible to tell if she was trying to refrain from crying or to keep from screaming in a fit of rage.

Finally, she nodded and said, "Yes, I understand."

\*\*\*

Mr. Podulski leaned on the desk that was meant for someone a fraction his age. He smiled and looked around at the empty room.

"I'm going to ask you a series of questions. I want the response you wouldn't dare admit to anyone else. I won't judge anything you say. Not a thing. Do you understand?"

Shelly finally resettled in her chair, still not quite recovered following Mr. Podulski's initial off-putting words. She pulled at the collar of her suit jacket even though it was exactly where it should be.

After she exhaled, she said, "I'll be completely honest with you, Mr. Podulski."

It was the first true thing she had said that week.

\*\*\*

Mr. Podulski's eyes went down the page of notes in front of him. "You're against a school dress code, is that correct?"

"Yes, I think everyone deserves to be allowed to wear whatever—"

"A simple yes or no will suffice."

"Yes."

"Would you be willing to switch your position if it meant the difference between getting elected or not?"

When Shelly's response wasn't immediate, the Economics teacher looked up from the paper. The eraser at the end of his pencil tapped against the desk.

Shelly's eyes narrowed. "Yes."

Mr. Podulski nodded. It was the response he had heard many times before from other kids who went on to become senior class president. And it was the answer he expected from her.

"Would you be willing to get someone expelled?"

The response was faster this time. "Of course."

"Would you be willing to ruin someone's future?"

Shelly pursed her lips. Her cell phone began to chime. The ring tone was the latest Justin Bieber song even though she despised the singer. It was only set to that damn song because when she was around other kids she wanted to seem... normal. Now, though, she jabbed at the SILENT button without looking at who was calling.

"Yeah," she said. "I would."

Mr. Podulski scribbled a couple of notes on the paper in front of him. Shelly leaned forward to see what he was writing but it was too small for her to read.

His final question was, "Is there anything you wouldn't do to become senior class president?"

Either she would say the right thing and he would be able to get her elected, or she would say the wrong thing and he would know the Traditionalists might have a chance after all. It didn't matter if she squirmed in her seat before she spoke the word or if she blushed at the thought of all the things that might be required of her or even if she smiled at the idea of finally paying back her enemies.

"No."

Mr. Podulski smiled and nodded. "Very good, Ms. McMarton. So this is how it will work then. You'll have a group of students supporting your run for senior class president. They'll do most of the work for you. All you have to do is smile and not get in the way of the machine."

Shelly thought she must have made some kind of

noise because Mr. Podulski stopped writing on his paper and looked up, eyes expectant, waiting for her to finish whatever it was she had to say before he could continue with the business at hand.

"I..." she said, looking around the room as if suddenly wishing class would begin so she would be saved. "I... don't have any friends to do that."

She expected him to say, "Not a single one?" or "Surely you know *someone* who would be willing to help you." Instead, he smiled and scribbled another note on the paper—that damn paper.

"You needn't worry, Ms. McMarton. I've taken the liberty of assembling a team of supporters on your behalf. We have"—his eyes scanned down toward the bottom of his notes—"roughly a dozen students who are going to help you with your campaign."

An involuntary smile washed over her face. Twelve students were going to volunteer their time on her behalf when they could be playing video games or texting.

"Who?"

"Deb Swasher, Mindy Peluso, Chrissy—"

Shelly blinked with surprise. Mr. Podulski was in the middle of naming a third student, but she couldn't help but interrupt.

"I hate Deb Swasher. I can't stand her. She laughed at me when I didn't win the sophomore debates last year."

The Economics teacher let out a long sigh. "Are you done?"

"Yeah."

"Deb Swasher doesn't like you either. You should have heard the things she said about you."

"What'd she say?" Shelly snapped.

No doubt, another name would have to be added to her little black book.

"That's not important. What is important is that she's willing to help get you elected."

"But why?"

Shelly's face puckered when she asked the question. She hated, absolutely despised, depending on someone else to tell her what she didn't know. It was part of the reason she was so passive-aggressive with most of her teachers.

"I thought you understood, Ms. McMarton." Podulski shook his head in disbelief. "None of this is about you. Deb and Nancy and the others are doing it for themselves."

"But what are they going to get out of it?"

"You'll appoint one to be the senior class vice president. You'll appoint another to be treasurer. A few of the kids are doing it because their parents agreed to buy them new cars if they helped you."

"Oh."

"Don't sound disappointed. It's the nature of the beast. I'm sure whoever the Traditionalists get behind will also have a team of students supporting him, very few of whom will genuinely like the kid they're supporting. It's how these things work."

Shelly's face was a ball of doubt. It took her a while to ask Mr. Podulski how he would ever hope to get her elected if even her supporters didn't actually like her.

"It's simple," he said and offered a big smile. "All we have to do is make your opponent seem even worse."

"Oh."

# 4

On the other side of the school, Chet Booth was also meeting with his faculty advisor for the first time.

Carl Stove taught U.S. History. In one of his lesson plans he discussed how the country had never lost a war. It was up to each student, many years later, to realize that they might have to figure out which parts of Stove's class hadn't been concerned with historical truth.

Mr. Stove was fat. The extent of his obesity made it impossible to refer to his weight in nicer terms. His face was wider than it was tall because of his massive red cheeks. His optometrist had to have special frames made for his glasses so they would fit around Stove's face. He had a way of gasping when he spoke, as if each breath were a marathon.

Chet didn't knock on Mr. Stove's door before entering. No act of polite announcement was necessary as far as he was concerned because Mr. Stove was there to help him get elected. As such, the honor was Stove's, not Chet's.

That wasn't to say Chet disliked Mr. Stove. Quite the opposite, he respected the U.S. History teacher for not seeking the friendship or acceptance of the other faculty members. Stove knew the other teachers hoped he would retire, and each day he showed up to United Exceptionalism he enjoyed seeing them disappointed that he was back for another day. In that regard, Chet and Mr. Stove were two peas in the same pod. Ever since Chet had read *A Separate Peace*, he had realized that wanting to be liked was a sign of weakness.

He acted upon this belief by refusing to compromise on anything at all. At the birthday party of one of his classmates, Chet had refused to wear shorts, sandals, and a Hawaiian shirt as the invitation had requested. The theme of the birthday, after all, was *Beach Party!* Instead, Chet told the boy's mother—a middle-aged woman who thought it was absolutely hilarious that someone would arrive to the party in loafers and dress pants—that he would either attend the party as he was dressed or not at all.

"Fine," the mother had said with a shrug.

When Chet had started past her toward the party, she had put a hand on his shoulder and stopped him.

"No, I meant, 'Fine, go home then.'"

The joke was on them. Instead of singing Happy Birthday to a kid he didn't even like, Chet went back to his house and carried out a massively successful raid against one of his many *World of Warcraft* arch enemies.

\*\*\*

Booth's stubborn nature extended to his daily life at school. It was either his way or no way at all, which was the primary reason nobody liked him. He was easy enough to get along with in one-on-one conversations. Even with his persistent awkward smile, which no one could look directly at, the other kids would admit there was nothing inherently wrong with Chet. That was, not until he attempted to single-handedly subvert each school function if he disagreed with a single aspect of it.

The freshman-sophomore school dance was supposed to be held out on the academy's golf course instead of inside the largest gymnasium or at the local country club. The vast majority of the students loved the idea. But Chet knew how much he would perspire if he had to sit on the seventh fairway for three hours. His already greasy face would become its own water trap. Instead of going along with what had been decided, Chet led an effort to have the entire dance cancelled if it was going to be held outside. He had almost no support but he was loud, adamant, and persistent. It looked as though the entire dance was going to be cancelled, and it almost had been. At the very last minute, Chet gave in and the dance went on.

"You're a real asshole," Jessica Buttron said to him, her friends nodding in agreement.

It was hard for him to take them seriously because they were all wearing shiny gowns. But Chet was particularly dismissive of them because they obviously had no clue what they were talking about. He had magnanimously allowed the dance to go on as planned despite his reservations; they should be thanking him rather than chastising him.

He did the same thing for a school field trip to Europe. Chet thought field trips should either be to museums or historic churches. Any other destination was a travesty, and he let it be known how much he disapproved. Once again, only a handful of other students agreed with him but that small group raised hell. At one point, he stood up in the cafeteria during lunch, right in front of the ice cream stand, and railed endlessly about the dangers of overseas field trips, ensuring no one got ice cream that day.

It went without saying that it would be a tall order to get him elected.

\*\*\*

"Let's talk," Stove said with a wheeze.

Unlike Mr. Podulski, Stove stayed at his desk while Chet took a seat at one of the student desks. Chet knew it was because there was no way Stove would fit somewhere else.

"Describe yourself in one sentence," Stove said.

Chet's eyes lit up at the chance to talk about himself. "I'm smart, realistic, devoted, and well-read." Chet fell silent for a moment, saw Stove was about to say something else, then added, "And I'm funny. Not in your usual dumb teenage way, but I'm constantly making my parents laugh. And I'm good at impersonations. The kids around here don't get my jokes but literary types love them. And I'm not much for sports or anything outdoors. And I don't like animals."

Stove closed his eyes and groaned.

"Okay, I think we have enough to start with."

Chet noticed his advisor wasn't writing any of this down. In fact, Stove didn't even have a pencil or paper on his desk. Chet thought everything he said should be written down, captured for the sake of United Exceptionalism's own chronicles. He frowned when he noticed that wouldn't be the case.

Mr. Stove's eyes scanned Chet's polished shoes and his shirt that was buttoned all the way to the collar.

"I gather from how you're dressed and from how outspoken you are that you're in favor of a strict dress code—maybe a return to students wearing uniforms. Is that correct?"

"Of course. The academy made a terrible decision getting rid of the dress code. That's not the type of institution the academy's founders had in mind."

Mr. Stove stared at Chet without blinking. "Would you be willing to switch your position if it meant the difference between getting elected or not?"

There was absolutely no pause in Chet's response. "Of course not. The problem isn't what I believe. The problem is that the rest of the student body doesn't agree with me. But I'm confident that if I can just get the opportunity to explain my side of things, they'll come around."

The history teacher took in a long, deep breath. Already, he was beginning to sweat through his shirt and the sun was only barely rising over the tops of the trees bordering the academy to the north.

"Let me get this right. Even if they agreed with you on every single other topic, you wouldn't be willing to modify your stance on the dress code? Do you realize how unrealistic that is considering the school is divided into thirds?"

In addition to the Traditionalists and the Reformists, there was another group of students and parents. A third of the students didn't care about the blind bias of the other two groups. These were the people who simply wanted a good education. The parents didn't really care who got elected senior class president as long as their children were learning and would attend a top college. Their kids didn't care which of their classmates got elected as long as they could endure the harsh daily realities of being a teenager.

Mr. Stove said, "How in blazes do you ever hope to appeal to more than just the dedicated Traditionalists if you aren't willing to be flexible?"

Chet blinked in confusion. "I already told you. Why aren't you listening? The kids need to come around to see it my way, not the other way around."

Stove chuckled. "I'll agree with one thing."

"What's that?" Chet asked.

"You do have a sense of humor that only adults can enjoy."

Chet brought a hand up to his mouth and began to nibble on a fingernail. It was one of his nervous habits that he was aware of but couldn't help. Sniffing his fingers after wiping sweat off his face was another. Refusing to leave a girl alone, even when she made it clear she despised him and wanted him to get away from her was another.

"Okay," Stove said, looking at the clock to see how much time they had left. "Is there anything, besides changing your stance on any topic, that you wouldn't be willing to do?"

"Like murder someone?"

Stove closed his eyes. "Let's think a bit less dramatic for now. Would you be willing to get someone kicked out of school?"

Chet thought of all the kids who had wanted that

dumb dance to be held on the golf course, all the students who wanted to go to London instead of the natural history museum.

"Yeah."

"Would you be willing to ruin someone's future?"

Chet pursed his lips. As far as he was concerned, the students' had already ruined their own futures by deciding to wear shorts and T-shirts to class instead of uniforms. After that, anything that happened was their own fault.

"Sure."

"Good. That's good to hear." When Stove nodded, his big cheeks bounced up and down. "Okay, give me a day to think about how best to approach this. We're going to need a miracle to get the kids to vote for you."

"Hey, what's that supposed to mean?"


# 5


While Chet Booth wasn't the only Traditionalist interested in running for senior class president, he was the only one who arrived in time for his first class. It was more important for Reginald Cript to watch some television and get his hair just right.

*** 

Many children had lemonade stands when they were in elementary school, selling lemonade made with real lemons squeezed into a glass and mixed with water and sugar. For his stand Cript claimed to use rare lemons imported from South America and exotic sugar substitutes. Instead of a quarter, Cript's cost five dollars.

He also spent a couple days delivering newspapers. Before he started, he made his father buy him a new bike that cost well over a thousand dollars. The backpack he bought for the job was also exorbitantly expensive.

Between sixth and seventh grade, Cript sold magazines door to door. Between eighth and ninth grade, he helped people get their lawns mowed. He didn't do the mowing himself, of course. Rather, he found people who needed their lawns managed and then hired homeless guys to walk across town and push the mowers. Cript would give them lunch and some drinks and pocket the money.

Each of these business interests eventually failed. No one would pay five dollars for a glass of lemonade, especially not one that turned out to be made from ordinary lemons and sugar. That was the first time he was accused of misrepresentation.

The newspaper route would have kept him employed but he hated getting up early, detested working up a sweat as he biked down the street. The thousand-dollar bike sat in the garage and gathered dust.

It got worse. The magazines he sold turned out to have been stolen. Someone had grabbed a stack of magazines from the store and mixed in some old copies taken from the library. When confronted, Cript swore the person who gave him the magazines in the first place must have done it. Who was that person? A man wearing an overcoat with the hood pulled over his head, preventing Cript from seeing his face. Or so Reginald said. Most assumed the man didn't exist.

Cript came closest to getting in trouble for hiring the homeless men and then paying them with peanut butter and jelly sandwiches instead of money. When the police asked what he thought he was doing, Reginald gave his patented combination of shrug and grin. His father made sure no charges were pressed.

# The Faulty Process of Electing a Senior Class President

***

None of these failures deterred Cript from greater and greater ambitions. To him, the lack of previous success didn't mean he was a failure because any time people were talking about him it was a good thing. What mattered was that everyone had heard of Cript Lemonade, Cript Lawn Care, and everything else he put his name on.

That was probably where the initial seed was planted in his brain to run for senior class president. During the election, every hallway and every classroom would be plastered with colored posters with his last name in big, bold letters. It was a chance for him to see his name in every hallway, every class, even inside the girl's bathrooms. People still talked about his other ventures even though they had been short-lived. If he could actually become senior class president, his name would never be forgotten.

It didn't cross his mind a single time that he knew nothing about what the senior class president actually did or the issues United Exceptionalism faced. Those things could be figured out later.

***

At first, no one took Cript's interest in becoming senior class president seriously. Rightfully so. He had never expressed any appreciation for school politics, didn't seem concerned with what happened at the academy, and spent all of his time chasing girls and spending his father's money. He was more devoted to managing the mop of blond hair atop his head than he was to voicing an opinion on the academy's dress code.

All summer he had said he was interested in the role and all summer the other kids had laughed. To the average student, the idea of a loudmouth like Cript besting the children of the most dignified Traditionalist families seemed absurd. But as soon as another student would voice his or her intention to run for senior class president, Cript would let out a volley of insults that brought most of them to tears. A few challenged Reginald to a fight, but he had effectively quashed their hopes for being the Traditionalist candidate—before their campaign had even begun.

When Jan Shrub, Jorge's little brother, hoped to repair the family name by becoming senior class president himself, Cript stood on a sofa at a party they were both at and went on a tirade.

"You're weak. You throw a baseball like a girl. Honestly, you might be a girl. Someone check Jan's shorts and see if he has a vagina. I didn't even know you were at this party until someone convinced me you were. You're so quiet no one knew you were here. I bet a kid five bucks that you weren't here because no one had seen your face or heard you say a word. It's probably better that way for you, quite frankly. Your brother was a moron who got the school into trouble, but at least he had a personality."

The harangue went on for over twenty minutes while everyone else laughed. No one else had ever really taken Jan's interest in becoming senior class president seriously because of the slogan he said he was going to use. Most candidates picked something like *Making United Exceptionalism Great Again!* or *The Candidate You Can Trust.* Jan Shrub said his slogan was simply going to be *Jan!* That was the first indication that Jorge's little brother wouldn't fare well.

By the time Cript was done mocking him, little Jan Shrub, his face the color of a spoiled orange, put his head down and left the party. He never expressed interest in running for senior class president again.

A week later, Cript heard someone talking about how Leslie H'Ounce might run for senior class president. At a party that weekend, Cript went out on the second-story deck of the house that overlooked a country club and went on a similar rant.

"They say Leslie H'Ounce might want to run for senior class president. Can you believe that? Leslie fucking H'Ounce. That kid's face is covered with so many zits I thought he had a yearlong case of chicken pox. Have you seen it? And he has a voice like he's been kicked in the nuts a million times. I heard a story—I don't know if this is true—but I heard someone saw him jerking off and his dick was so small he had to use just his index finger and thumb. And that kid wants to be senior class president?"

That outburst only lasted five minutes because a girl at the party went out on the deck and whispered into Cript's ear, "Leslie's gone. He couldn't take it anymore and left."

Cript, satisfied at another job well done, went back and got another drink.

The summer progressed that way until the school year began and Chet Booth was the only Traditionalist still left in Cript's way.

# 6

The first week of school passed without any major developments. The kids went to their classes. The teachers got a sense of which students would study hard, which would turn in late or incomplete work, and which would disrupt class. The janitors scraped gum off the bleachers. The kitchen staff made shrimp tacos and custom pizzas and crab sandwiches.

None of the kids arrived to United Exceptionalism in the mornings hoping for more details about who would be senior class president because almost none of them cared. The students were focused on the things that actually mattered to them, like their homework, who had just broken up with whom, and avoiding saying or doing anything that would bring them unwanted attention.

In many ways, Yeri and Anna were the typical students at United Exceptionalism. Each lived in a nice house that their parents had no problem affording. Both would be able to attend just about any college they wanted.

The couple had only been dating for three months but already the two juniors were proclaiming their love for each other. Even though they lived down the street from each other, they had never spoken to one another until waiting in line to use the same bathroom at a party over the summer. Until then, Yeri had assumed Anna was egotistical because she never said hello to him and Anna assumed Yeri had something against her because he never acknowledged her. Standing in silence as other kids went into and out of the bathroom, they eventually struck up a conversation and soon realized they had both been completely wrong about the other.

They spent the rest of the night talking and the rest of the summer doing everything together. Before that party, they had devoted all of their time to hanging out with friends. Afterward, their friends rarely saw them. If they were awake, Anna and Yeri were either writing each other notes, talking on the phone, texting, holding hands, or making out. In short, they were typical lovestruck teenagers.

***

While Anna and Yeri transitioned from summer romance to school-year couple, the wheels of the machine that was the election for senior class president began to turn.

One of the cheerleaders was overheard telling her friends that Shelly McMarton was the only logical choice, not just as the Reformist candidate, but as senior class president. No one knew she was saying this because her father, a prominent Reformist alumnus who owned one of the area's largest companies, had promised to buy her a new car if she helped get Shelly elected.

The leader of the debate team told his buddies that everything about Shelly's life had been in preparation for becoming senior class president and he would be shocked if anyone voted for someone else. As he was a skilled debater, none of the other kids doubted the validity of his argument. Little did they know his mother had promised to introduce him to a reality TV star he had a crush on—a young woman who was famous for a sex tape and for embarrassing herself on a weekly show—if her son helped get Shelly elected.

A freshman, a girl with aspirations of running for senior class president in a couple years, told all of her friends that she was proud to call Shelly a friend and that the academy would be in good hands with her as president. The girl only said this because she wanted to be in Shelly's place in a couple years and needed to get on Mr. Podulski's good side as soon as possible.

The friends of these students didn't take the comments they overheard seriously. Each kid simply thought they were hearing honest opinions of Shelly McMarton. None of them realized their friends had the incentive of a new car or a Caribbean vacation or something else. Slowly but surely, every student heard someone else say that Shelly was the inevitable choice for senior class president. All of them realized it wasn't a matter of *if* McMarton would be elected, but *when*.

\*\*\*

Some of the same machinations unfolded with the Traditionalists, but not nearly as much because of the poor quality of the candidates. Chet Booth's advisor lobbied some of the Traditionalist parents for support, but it wasn't easy. Who could get people excited about a kid who had tried to get a school dance cancelled?

The Traditionalist alumni wanted a senior class president who shared their beliefs, but the students they would have liked to support were already out of the race because of Reginald Cript. Left with the choice of supporting Booth, Cript, or doing nothing, only a few chose to support Chet. The others couldn't yet bring themselves to support a boy whose mere photograph made them shudder in disgust and whose voice was like fingernails clawing a chalkboard.

***

Cript had none of the same alliances working for him. Instead, he relied on being loud and abrasive. One of his favorite tactics was to stand on top of one of the tables in the cafeteria and go on long rants about other students. Most of the time, he tore apart other candidates who had already dropped out of the race. Everyone nearby laughed and waited to hear what Cript would say next.

Each time he stood up on a lunch table, the cafeteria held its collective breath, each student hoping they weren't the next target of Cript's belligerent mockery, and then roaring with laughter to let Reginald know they appreciated him targeting another poor bastard instead. No one spoke up and told Reginald to stop because no one wanted to become his new target.

"I swear, the first time I saw Chet Booth I thought the elephant man had taken a shit, dressed it like a douchebag, and then sent it off to try and get all of our school dances cancelled. Talk about creepy, right? I swear, I'm not afraid of much, but just imagining waking up in the middle of the night and seeing that kid standing over me with that weird smile terrifies me!"

# The Faulty Process of Electing a Senior Class President

***

Anna and Yeri watched the way Cript belittled Booth and couldn't figure out how United Exceptionalism had ended up with such a poor slate of choices. Both of them had been freshmen when Jorge M. Shrub had sent the academy into a tailspin with his terrible decisions. And yet nothing much had changed in the years since. They saw with their own eyes the way the rest of the students at United Exceptionalism had grown disgruntled with the kids they elected to represent them. With the candidates lined up to become the next senior class president, nothing seemed likely to change during their last year at United Exceptionalism either.

Shelly was universally disliked for talking behind other students' backs and for lying about simple stuff she had no reason to fib about. Chet disdained the average student enough that he tried to cancel all of the events they liked. And Reginald got attention for acting like a bully.

As Cript continued his verbal assault on Chet, Yeri leaned over toward Anna and said, "Doesn't bode well for the future of the academy."

But what was the alternative to the fool shouting from the top of a cafeteria table? Someone they couldn't trust? Someone they had a visceral hatred for? All around Anna and Yeri were students who deserved someone who would work for them, give them the type of academy they actually wanted. Instead, Reginald was spewing hatred everywhere. Chet was a buffoon. Shelly wasn't telling anyone what she stood for or what she would do. Worse, there were rumors she wasn't a Reformist at all, but was merely saying what people wanted to hear in order to get elected.

The United Exceptionalism Academy for Boys and Girls was supposed to be the best school in the country. Were these really the best candidates available for senior class president?

It was almost enough to make a kid want to go to public school. Almost.

# 7

By the second week of classes, students had gotten into their routines and it was becoming another typical year at United Exceptionalism. For one reason or another, most of the people at the academy weren't happy with what the current senior class president was doing. But a freshman-sophomore dance was coming up. Shortly after that, a junior dance would be held. Then the senior dance. The football season was getting ready to begin. Life went on, and everyone was reassured that things would improve as soon as the next election was held.

Anna got in trouble with her parents for missing her curfew by half an hour and was grounded for one week. Without the ability to see his girlfriend after school, Yeri had to find something else to pass the time. His friends saw him for the first time in a month and, when they did, they teased him relentlessly about being on his girlfriend's leash. It was what happened to every couple at least once a year.

\*\*\*

Shelly McMarton spent more time planning what she would do once she became senior class president than she did studying. That's not to say she did poorly in her school work. As long as students actually attended classes, which she did, it was difficult not to do well at the academy. Most students got A's or B's with minimal effort.

When she was in class, she wasn't listening to the teacher talk about the periodic table or the causes of World War I or the themes in *Huckleberry Finn*. She was daydreaming about what it would be like when she was the senior class president. She would be the most powerful person at the academy. They wouldn't like her and she wouldn't like them, but they would have to act as though they liked her, and that power was what drove her to the office.

She still didn't talk to any of her classmates and they didn't talk to her. That was fine. All they had to do was check the appropriate box when election day came.

*** 

"I guess you've heard the news," Mr. Podulski said before class the next day.

Most students running for senior class president met with their faculty advisor once a week. Shelly met with hers every day just to make sure everything was going according to plan.

McMarton's eyes narrowed. "What news?"

The Economics professor motioned to a desk at the front of class. "Why don't you have a seat?"

"What news?" Shelly asked again. She put her book bag on the floor and scooted into a seat as the Economics teacher suggested.

Once she was seated, Mr. Podulski looked down at some scribbled notes on a piece of notebook paper and then tilted his gaze up to peer over the tops of his glasses.

"Do you know a boy named Percy Wethers?"

Shelly let out a single huffing scoff. "No, should I?"

"He's a junior."

"Okay."

Shelly stared at her faculty advisor and let her eyes drift closed as if she were already bored. A boy named

Percy was trivial to her.

"He's expressed interest in running for senior class president."

The response was much slower this time, the single word drawn out over the course of three seconds. "Okayyyyyy."

"As a Reformist."

Shelly's nostrils flared. A vein bulged at her left temple and another on the side of her neck. That part of her response was involuntary. On the other hand, every word that left her lips was calculated. It was said she didn't even tell her parents she loved them unless she first weighed the advantages and disadvantages of saying it on any given day. As angry as she was in that moment, she thought about what she could say without getting in trouble. After concluding that only Mr. Podulski, her most trusted ally, would hear, she gave the response she deemed appropriate to the situation.

"What the fuck?"

Then, her voice growing louder, screeching like the bell that signaled the end of one class and the beginning of another, "What the fucking fuck!"

\*\*\*

Shelly's hands closed into fists.

"Okay," Mr. Podulski said, "Take it easy."

"Take it easy?"

"Yes. No one's heard of this kid. He's not even a real Reformist as far as we can tell. It sounds like he's never expressed any interest in being considered a Reformist before. No one will care about him. No one will care whatever it is he has to say."

A pudgy teenage fist, its fingernails painted a dignified red, came smashing down on the desk.

"I was supposed to be the only Reformist! Everyone knew. Everyone knew it was supposed to be my year."

"And they still know it," Podulski soothed. "You're getting yourself excited over nothing."

"Over nothing?" Shelly yelled, her eyes widening with manic rage.

Mr. Podulski shook his head and held out a hand to quiet her. "I already have your helpers going around disparaging this Percy kid. His campaign for senior class president will be over before it begins."

Shelly's eyes softened, the first sign of a smile began to return to her face. "What are they saying?"

"The usual. That he's not actually a Reformist. That whatever he believes is nonsense and unrealistic. That he doesn't have a chance of beating you and shouldn't be taken seriously."

"Will it work?

"Of course. Before long, it'll be common knowledge that young Mr. Wethers is in over his head. When he realizes that for himself, you'll never hear from him again."

"Won't it make me look bad if they badmouth him?"

From the way her eyes scanned Mr. Podulski's face, it was obvious she wasn't concerned in whether or not Percy was torn down, only if the students at United Exceptionalism would think less of Shelly when it happened.

The Economics teacher chuckled without trying to hide his amusement.

"None of it will be connected to you. You don't talk to any of the students who are spreading these ideas anyway and they certainly don't talk to you. When a kid hears that Percy isn't a realistic choice and that you're the only possible candidate, they'll think of it as nothing more than a simple statement of truth."

"You've done this before?"

"Of course."

"And it works?"

Mr. Podulski smiled. "Every time."

# 8

It was true that almost no one knew who Percy Wethers was. It was also true that he didn't consider himself a Reformist. Unathletic, quiet, and oafish, Percy had few friends. He liked spending his time with headphones on and his eyes closed. The combination of not being able to see or hear others around him ensured he remained a social recluse.

The one time he didn't listen to music, other than during his classes, was at lunch. Instead of losing himself in his favorite songs, he watched and listened to the other kids. What he saw were students who just wanted to be happy, who wanted to mind their own business and worry about the things that ordinary teenagers cared about. They weren't interested in the football team being sent to another high school to terrorize the kids there. They weren't interested in arguing over school uniforms or jeans. They were more concerned with not doing or saying anything to get made fun of and hoping the boy or girl they had a crush on also liked them in return.

Percy also knew, from all the books he had read, that it was possible to improve United Exceptionalism in ways other senior class presidents wouldn't dare think of. For instance, he had learned that certain other schools provided each student with laptops to take to all of their classes. Everywhere this happened the students got higher marks and the teachers said the kids were able to learn faster. If that was true, why wasn't United Exceptionalism doing the same?

Even worse, he noticed Shelly McMarton wasn't saying what she would do for the school. Instead, she remained silent, refusing to provide her stance on any topic. There were rumors she had agreed with Jorge M. Shrub's decision to send the football team over to wreak havoc at Iroquois Regional High School. Sometimes she said she was for the dress code and other times she was against it. It was impossible to know what she really believed.

\*\*\*

He started his campaign for senior class president the old-fashioned way. Instead of posting his intention on Twitter or Facebook, he overheard a girl complain to her friends about how much the academy charged for her textbooks. And then told her what he would do about it.

"It'd be nice if I had enough of my parent's money leftover to at least go shopping," the girl said.

She was with seven of her friends, at the lunch table next to where he was sitting by himself. She wore a long, bright yellow sundress. All of the girls at the table gestured with their hands whenever they laughed or said something sarcastic, which was almost constantly.

"If that wasn't bad enough, my dad's on my last nerve with all this computer bullshit." The girl in the bright yellow sundress lowered her voice and gave a mock expression of extreme seriousness. "Kathy, I didn't buy you this computer so you could play around all the time. You need to start doing more chores around the house."

A girl across the table from her said, "Fucking old people."

"I know, right?"

"What if United Exceptionalism provided you with your own free laptop?" Percy asked. "Then you wouldn't be indebted to your dad."

That was how it started.

\*\*\*

The girls looked at each other in confusion as if an invisible boy were somehow intruding on their private conversation.

Finally, yellow sundress—Kathy—turned to Percy and asked, "Why would United Exceptionalism buy me a laptop?"

Her friends laughed as she posed the question, the mere words a mockery of the gawky boy with fair skin and thick glasses who was sitting by himself.

Rather than grow shy or pick up his tray and wander off embarrassed, Percy smiled.

"That's what they do at some other academies. They buy all the kids laptops and they end up getting better grades because of it."

Kathy narrowed her eyes, studying the boy at the table beside her.

One of the other girls whispered, "How long has he been sitting there?"

"Has he always been sitting there?" another asked in a hushed voice.

"Other academies are buying laptops for their students and this place isn't?" Kathy said, the only one speaking loud enough that Percy was actually supposed to be able to hear.

"Yeah," he said, his hair bouncing as his confidence increased. "They certainly do. And it works. Not to mention, if the school provided you with one, your dad wouldn't be able to hold it over your head."

The table of girls—four blonds, two brunettes, one redhead, and one with curly brown frizzes—stared at Percy, unsure of what to make of him.

"I'm going to be running for senior class president," he said with a grin. "And if I win, you'll have a nice new laptop the first day of class next year."

Kathy stared open-mouthed at the goofy boy. One of the football players walked by and tapped her on her opposite shoulder as he went past, hoping she would look the wrong way and find no one there. Instead, she kept gazing at the kid with the headphones around his neck and an open book beside his lunch tray.

"I love what you're saying," she said in a deadpan voice. "Tell me more."

He got the feeling she was doing an impression from some popular movie or TV show but he couldn't begin to guess which one it might be. Instead of bothering to ask, he told her and her friends all the other things he would do if he were elected.

\*\*\*

"Well, for one thing," he said, leaning forward, excited to have a chance to explain all of his ideas. "You'd be allowed to dress however you want."

A girl next to Kathy said, "We already got rid of the dress code."

"No, you got rid of school uniforms. You still have a dress code. There're still certain things you can wear and can't wear."

"Like what?"

"Like anything. If you want to wear a uniform you should be allowed to. If you want to go even more casual, you should be allowed to do that too. Like flip-flops. If you want to wear flip-flops, why shouldn't you be able to?"

"I freaking love flip-flops," one of the other girls at the table said.

Kathy, who seemed to be the girls' leader, asked, "What else?"

He didn't know if she meant, *What other clothes would we be allowed to wear?* or if she meant, *What other ideas do you have besides flip-flops and free laptops?* Not wanting to lose their interest, he blurted the first thing that came to his mind.

"Bras. You shouldn't have to wear bras if you don't want to."

Every set of eyes at the table across from him became twice as large. Every mouth dropped open. One of the girls, more developed than the others, subconsciously folded her arms in front of her chest.

Percy's heart stopped. His ears rang. He stared at Kathy, hoping for her to say something, anything. Instead, she burst out laughing. As soon as she did, the other girls joined in.

"Oh my god, you're a perv," she said, but there was no ill will behind her words because she could see he hadn't meant any harm.

"Not at all," he replied. "It's what women did back in the late sixties. My dad was there. He said it was about women having the right to wear whatever they wanted to wear. Equal rights, all that. You shouldn't have to wear one just because you're told to. Oh, and did I mention your textbooks would be cheaper? They cost a fraction of the price in other countries, you know. And why do we have a drinking fountain that keeps making kids sick? We need to fix that."

He put his water bottle up to his mouth and poured the entire contents down his throat. He put the cap back on the bottle and hoped that the girls wouldn't start making fun of him.

In the same monotone drawl as before, Kathy said, "You're blowing my mind, man."

\*\*\*

It wasn't all laughs and impersonations, though. One of the girls at the table had been recruited by Mr. Podulski to praise everything Shelly McMarton did. Of course, neither her friends nor Percy had any way of knowing that.

The girl said, "Who's going to pay for these laptops?" And then, tossing her hair to one side, added, "Huh, Mr. Smarty-pants?"

"Well, that's simple. Our parents."

Kathy sighed and shook her head. "Well, then my dad's still gonna get on my case."

"No, because it'll be built into the price of tuition. Tuition here is already more expensive than any other school. You're telling me it costs that much and they *can't* afford to buy us laptops? I think that's the travesty."

The same turncoat friend, her lipstick and eyeliner glistening, gave her friends a look of disbelief that let them know not to take Percy seriously.

"What proof do you have that laptops actually work in classrooms?"

"I read about it."

The girl snorted and shook her head in disbelief. "I've read a lot of things in books too. We all have. You ever read *Lord of the Flies*? Maybe we should kill each other just because we read about it in a book."

"It works, though," he insisted. "There have been studies—"

None of the other girls were listening anymore, however. Each of them had turned to face sparkly makeup to see what she would say next, and Percy knew that even if they had liked what he was saying there was something they would always like more: watching the cruelty that kids were capable of.

"You almost tricked me, Pervy Percy, with that talk of flip-flops and no bras. Didn't take you long to get down to business. I bet you've never even touched a boob."

The truth was he hadn't, but that wasn't what mattered. Whether he said he had or he hadn't was beside the point. Anything else he did say was going to be used against him.

# 9

The opposite was true of Cript, who could say anything he wanted and get away with it. He used his interest in running for senior class president as an excuse to ask out May Shallowstein. After she rejected him, he told her she was a fat pig and had no right to be a cheerleader. Instead of apologizing to her when she started to cry, he doubled down, badmouthing her until, in an odd twist of events, she apologized to him for not turning him down in a nicer manner.

It didn't matter that her initial rejection had been a simple, "No, thanks." It also didn't matter that she wasn't the least bit overweight. Only after the apology was delivered to him did Cript cease his taunts.

Rather than despise him for how he treated his fellow classmates, the other kids seemed to not only accept it but to hope they were nearby so they could overhear the next inappropriate yet funny thing he said.

*** 

Oddly, even though Cript saw that Shelly McMarton and Chet Booth both had faculty advisors, he still didn't think to ask for one of his own. Instead, he was happy to spend his days ripping apart Traditionalist students who had initially expressed interest in running for senior class president but who had since dropped out.

"I'll tell you something," Cript said, speaking loud enough for everyone within four lunch tables to hear. "Jan Shrub is the dumbest kid I think I've ever met in my entire life. The pizza I'm eating right now is smarter than that stupid son of a bitch. What's the difference between Jan Shrub and…" He paused, momentarily unable to think of another option, and then continued. "…and someone else?

At least someone else knows they have their head up their ass."

Leslie H'Ounce fared no better, even though he hadn't mentioned running for senior class president since halfway through summer.

"Leslie H'Ounce reminds me of that kid that shows up to school with a trench coat and a machine gun." He gave an impression of the sound of automatic gunfire. "That's one weird kid. Honestly, I think United Exceptionalism regrets letting him in. His own parents probably regret having him. Now that I think about it, he was probably an accident. Had to be an accident."

# 10

Rather than eat in the cafeteria with everyone else, Chet Booth sat in Mr. Stove's empty classroom. On the walls all around him were framed portraits of past senior class presidents at United Exceptionalism who had gone on to achieve fame or fortune in the real world.

"The problem," Stove said, his puffy cheeks a darker shade of red than usual, "is that people are having a hard time getting excited about you."

Chet cringed, betraying his forced smile. "Getting excited about me?"

"Yeah, I've been talking to some of the Traditionalist parents and none of them care for you. You tried to get their kids' dance cancelled, for god's sake. They don't like Cript either, but at least he's funny."

"I can be funny too. What did the bottle of ketchup say to the tomato?"

Stove sighed and took a mighty breath of air. "That's an old joke and you're not even telling it the right way. You ruined it, in fact."

Chet sank down in his chair. His loafers stuck out from the edge of the desk, each one shiny enough that the general form of his large face could be seen in their reflection.

"What do we do then?" Booth had already spent more than ten years in school trying to be likeable—or at the very least, not detestable—and had failed.

"Don't give up hope, my boy. I'll keep at it. Cript's a funny kid but not a realistic choice. The Traditionalists will come around and see you're the only reasonable option left."

Booth nodded and shuffled out from the side of the desk. He zipped up his backpack and looked at the clock above the doorway to see how much time he had before his next class.

"Oh, and one other thing, Chet?"

"Yeah?"

Mr. Stove let one side of his mouth curl into a grin while the other half remained inflexible. In the two weeks they had been working together, Booth had come to realize that this expression meant *You're not going to like me for saying this but...*

Stove said, "Stop looking people squarely in the eyes when you smile. It creeps the hell out of them."

\*\*\*

What followed wasn't pretty. Chet Booth set about making it his mission to get people to like him. He would be the opposite of Cript. Instead of assaulting them with words, Booth would laugh at everything they said. Instead of mocking them, he would be just like them. He could wait to convince them that his vision for United Exceptionalism was the right one. The important thing right now was to endear himself to all of the students and teachers.

\*\*\*

The next day, he brought a duffel bag to school filled with clothes, gear, and teenage necessities. During lunch, when some of the boys were known to sneak off for a smoke break, Chet grabbed a brand new leather jacket out of the bag, put it on, and suddenly decided he had to use the same bathroom the smokers used.

"Oh, hey guys," he said as he gave a nonchalant shrug and shouldered past them on his way to a urinal.

His coat still smelled like the store it had been purchased from the day before. If it weren't for the smoke that pervaded the bathroom, the entire area would have stunk like the leather coat store or the urinal cakes the janitor had put in the previous day.

One of the kids replied with a grunt and then took a drag off his cigarette.

Chet expected them to ask if he'd like to take a smoke as well. He didn't know what he would say if they did ask. He hadn't gotten that far in his planning. But even though he swore he would never put a death stick in his mouth, he figured he would do it now if it meant these boys would vote for him. Instead, the smokers ignored him.

Chet finished and began toward the door.

"Wash your hands, you dirty motherfucker," one of the older boys said.

"Oh, I never wash my hands. The faucet handles have too many germs on them." He said it with a huge smile, thinking he had made a valid point.

In return, though, one of the other kids said, "I'm never borrowing a pencil from that kid. His dick germs will be on it."

Not knowing what else to say, Chet grinned and left. The leather coat he had been wearing went right back into the duffel bag.

\*\*\*

In its place, he withdrew a pair of jogging shoes, a pair of shorts, and a T-shirt. He despised this type of clothing but he knew it was vital to being seen as an ordinary kid, so he did what he never imagined himself capable of. After the final bell rang, he went for a jog on the school track.

It was worse than he could have imagined. Having never run from point A to point B in his life, having never played organized sports or backyard football, he had no idea how taxing it was to jog. He was huffing for breath before he was halfway around the first lap.

Three boys were there, stretching before they started their own run. A group of four girls was sitting in the bleachers talking. All of them, the boys included, giggled as Chet ran around the track. His arms flailed. His feet moved in stomping strides. It dawned on him that no one had ever taught him how to run before.

"Nice day out, huh?" he said to the boys who were stretching.

He was breathing so hard, though, gasping for air, that he wasn't sure if his words were intelligible.

"Have you ever been allowed out of your parents' basement?" one of the kids called back.

"Yeah," Chet said, "Why?"

"It's just that you're so goddamned pale."

The boy's friends both laughed. The girls, also hearing it, giggled louder than they had upon first seeing Booth in his outfit.

\*\*\*

The next day, Anna and Yeri were holding hands and talking by Anna's locker when Chet appeared from the nearest entryway. He was wearing overalls and a straw hat.

The outfit was made more ridiculous by the fact that Chet still had on his shiny loafers.

"Howdy," Chet said as he walked past them.

Part of Anna wanted to laugh; this was one of the two boys vying to be the Traditionalist candidate for senior class president. Another part of her wanted to cry; this was one of the two boys vying to be the Traditionalist candidate for senior class president.

Yeri refused to blink. He was afraid that the apparition that had been a country version of Chet Booth might disappear, and he wanted to enjoy it for as long as it lasted.

All he managed to say was, "I can't believe it's either going to be him or Reginald Cript."

# 11

The academy wasn't far into the school year before the school newspaper began covering the four students running for senior class president. United Exceptionalism didn't bother with a print version of the articles they produced—that version of *The Representative* had been done away with a decade earlier. Instead, they kept a website updated with the various articles written by student contributors, each of which were also tweeted out to the students and posted to *The Representative's* Facebook page for the entire student body to read when they had absolutely nothing else to do.

Although it wouldn't be known until a year later (and by then, no one would care) the editor of *The Representative*, a senior named Chrissy Cassidy, had been recruited by Mr. Podulski to support McMarton. In Chrissy's case, she went along with it because a Reformist alumnus who ran a television station let it be known that if Chrissy admirably performed her duties as editor of the school paper, she would have a paid internship waiting for her after she graduated.

It was an easy choice to make.

\*\*\*

A different student would interview each candidate and then write an article about them. The first student was a junior named Hannah Morganson. She was tasked with speaking to Shelly McMarton.

"I'd like to interview you for *The Representative*," Hannah said, smiling, excited to be allowed to skip her usual class for this assignment.

Shelly was sitting at a computer in the corner of the academy library. She turned and looked at the girl standing over her.

"You are?"

"Hannah. Hannah Morganson. I'm writing for *The Representative*. We're doing a series of interviews and—"

"Talk to Mr. Podulski," Shelly said, already turning back to the monitor. "He can speak on my behalf."

Hannah's smile flickered. "But it's to help you get elected. It's to let the school know where you stand on important topics."

"Yeah, I get that," Shelly said, not bothering to look away from the computer screen. "I'm busy, though. Please go away."

"I..."

But seeing that Shelly had no intention of talking to her or even looking in her direction, Hannah picked up her bag and left.

\*\*\*

After school that day, Hannah leaned her head

inside Mr. Podulski's empty Economics classroom. Podulski looked up from the papers he was grading and squinted at her.

"Yes?"

"I'm writing for *The Representative*. I'm doing a piece about Shelly McMarton."

"Of course!" He pushed the stack of papers away and put the cap back on the red pen he had been using to scribble marks on each quiz. "Come in, come in."

Hannah sat at the desk closest to Mr. Podulski and pulled out a notepad.

She had a set of questions she was going to ask but she started by mumbling, "I tried to talk with Shelly in the library but she wouldn't speak to me."

Mr. Podulski laughed the comment away and then, for good measure, also swatted the imaginary words with his hand.

"She's extremely busy, I'm sure you can imagine. Running for senior class president and the charity she works on and whatnot."

"But I'm trying to get her exposure."

Mr. Podulski sighed and shook his head the way he did when an underclassman was wasting his time.

"Like I said, she's extremely busy, but I can help you with your article."

Hannah wondered what was going to happen when she turned in her interview and didn't have a single quote by the person she was supposed to be speaking with. Cringing, she opened her notebook and readied her pen underneath the first pre-written question.

"Why are you running for senior class president?"

She immediately realized her mistake and her cheeks turned red. Mr. Podulski smiled, but didn't otherwise acknowledge it.

"Shelly is running for senior class president because she thinks she's the best person for the job and because the role requires someone with her level of experience. No one can argue she's the most qualified candidate."

"The other students don't believe anything she says, though. How will she earn their trust?"

The smile on Mr. Podulski's face faded and his expression turned to barely restrained scorn. He let out an audible sigh to let Hannah know this type of question wasn't worthy of *The Representative*.

"Trust is overrated. Experience counts for much more. And what you'll find is that Shelly is the most qualified candidate this academy has ever seen. That's why she has the support of nearly every teacher and every Reformist alumnus."

"But she supported Jorge M. Shrub sending the football team to beat up the kids at Iroquois Regional High School."

"No, I think you're mistaken," Podulski said.

Hannah flipped a couple pages further into her binder to find some notes she had taken.

"When it happened, she told Anne Durbin that, and I quote, 'They had what was coming to them. I would have done the same thing.' End of quote."

"Who's Anne Durbin?"

"She graduated last year."

Mr. Podulski shook his head and rolled his eyes. "Well, if she's not here, I don't see why her opinion matters."

"It wasn't her opinion. It was a quote of what Shelly said."

Mr. Podulski smiled, but he didn't blink when he did so, which reminded Hannah of how her father looked when he got home from work after a particularly rough day.

Mr. Podulski's response summed up the expression: "Next question."

"Shelly has also said a couple times since then that she could envision sending the football team to beat up kids at other schools."

Mr. Podulski's hands came up in the air in an exaggerated manner. "Maybe they had it coming. Are you going to say it's never okay for the football team to beat up kids? Come on, this is the real world."

"She also went back and forth on whether she supported the dress code, depending on who she was talking to."

"These are complex issues. It's perfectly understandable to change your position as you learn more about a topic."

\*\*\*

That night, Hannah typed up her article. It began:

*While nobody can deny that Shelly McMarton possesses the experience necessary to become senior class president, serious questions persist about her stance on a variety of issues and how she would deal with key events if she were elected.*

\*\*\*

"What's this?" Chrissy Cassidy was scanning the draft in front of her, holding it with the edge of her fingertips as if it would infect her.

"My interview with Shelly. She didn't want to talk to me, though, so I interviewed her faculty advisor instead." Thinking that was the reason for Chrissy's attitude, she added, "But he answered all of my questions and—"

"Whatever."

Seeing that Chrissy was done with her, Hannah left.

\*\*\*

After editing, the first article from *The Representative* began:

> *Nobody can deny that Shelly McMarton possesses the experience necessary to serve as senior class president. Her faculty advisor even went as far as to say that this was a key reason in the nearly unanimous support she has from faculty and alumni alike. Shelly possesses the firm response this academy deserves. She possesses the resilience this institution needs.*

# 12

Prior to developing a crush on Hannah Morganson, Brian Toppert had never expressed any interest in writing for *The Representative*. After he found out Hannah was writing articles for the school paper, he suddenly became interested in journalism.

His first assignment was to interview Percy Wethers.

"Who?"

"Exactly," Chrissy Cassidy said, for once actually tolerating an underclassman.

"No, seriously, does he go to this school?"

"Of course, idiot."

"I've never heard of him before."

"There's probably a lot you don't know, Brian. I wouldn't go around advertising the fact."

\*\*\*

After the day's classes were finished, Brian found Percy in the school cafeteria. He expected to see someone with a strong jaw and nicely combed hair, a boy that looked like he was ripped from the pages of an Abercrombie & Fitch advertisement. The person he saw was the furthest thing from that expectation that United Exceptionalism had ever admitted as a student. Even hunched over the table and reading a book, Percy looked big enough to be in college rather than high school. His hair, an uncombed tangle of blond strings, looked like it was already thinning.

The boy was so engrossed in whatever he was reading that he didn't notice Brian until they were sitting at the same table.

"Hello?" Brian said, already opening his backpack and pulling out some paper.

Percy turned and beamed a large smile. "Thanks for coming to talk to me. I appreciate it."

"I have to admit, I didn't know your name before this assignment."

Percy smiled again and nodded. "I get that a lot."

With a pen and paper ready, Brian said, "Okay, so you want to be senior class president?"

"I do."

"Why?"

Percy leaned back in his seat. Then, realizing the chair didn't have a backrest to put his weight against, he clutched at the edge of the table to save himself from an embarrassing fall.

Upright and steadied, he said, "I love this academy. It has a rich history and we do a lot of good things here. But we can do better. That should always be our goal."

"And you want to do that by giving each kid a free laptop?"

Rather than take offense, Percy nodded excitedly. "Absolutely. Listen, this is something they're already doing in other private schools. And it works. Why wouldn't we do it too then, just because we didn't think of it first? This academy does wonderful things, and I'm as proud of it as anyone else, but I want to be proud of it finding new ways to support its students. Is that so crazy?"

Brian was scribbling notes as he listened. After receiving the assignment to interview Percy, he had asked around and soon learned of the "Free Laptop Kid" who was running for senior class president. Other candidates were worried about the dress code and inter-school fights and here was some oafish boy going on about free laptops for everyone like United Exceptionalism was some kind of utopian school.

"You know, that'll cost *a lot* of money."

"It already costs a lot to go here. This is an expensive school. For that tuition we get a nice golf course, we pay for all the damage the football team causes to other schools, we get lawyers who pay to make sure the team and Jorge M. Shrub don't get sent to juvie. I don't need to tell you there are much better ways to spend our tuition. Why not get kids the laptops they need to learn more effectively? While we're at it, why don't we stop sending the football team to beat people up? Does that sound *sooo* crazy?"

After scribbling more notes, Brian looked down at his next question. A smirk spread across his face.

"And, you want girls to go braless?"

Percy shook his head and waved the comment away. "We can have fun and joke about it but I don't care if they go braless or not. What I care about is that we've made progress by moving away from school uniforms. Why stop there? Why not wear flip-flops if you want?"

Brian jotted down the response and put his pen aside. He had come to the interview without much hope that some kid he had never heard of before would say something interesting. Now that he was here, though, he wasn't laughing.

"Okay, so what else?"

"Well, the price of textbooks is outrageous. The companies selling the books are getting rich off our students. Did you know academies in other countries pay a fraction for the exact same books we buy for hundreds of dollars? And why isn't anyone fixing the water fountain that keeps making kids sick? No one else even talks about it."

\*\*\*

This is how Brian started his article when he got home:

*At various tables around the cafeteria, at lockers between classes, excitement is slowly building. Students are talking about flip-flops and free laptops and cheaper textbooks. The reason for that is a little-known junior named Percy Wethers. While few students knew who he was two weeks ago, his ideas are starting to be taken seriously. Percy will be the first to tell you that everything he proposes is already improving other schools where the same policies have been adopted.*

\*\*\*

This is how the first article from *The Representative* began after Chrissy Cassidy edited it:

*At various tables around the cafeteria, at lockers between classes, kids are trying to figure out who Percy Wethers is and why they should care. His response to the latter? Because he reads books. While Shelly McMarton, Reginald Cript, and Chet Booth may not agree on many things, at least they're talking about realistic solutions to what's ailing United Exceptionalism. Should you take Percy's ideas seriously? Percy recently said, "I don't care if they (girls) go braless or not." It sounds as if the answer may be a resounding NO.*

# 13

Jordan Sustabal also wrote for *The Representative*, but not because he had a crush on Hannah Morganson. He wrote for the school paper because his best friend, Brian Toppert, did have a crush on Hannah and, not having anything better to do with his time, he decided he might as well see which other girls worked there.

Jordan's first assignment was an interview with Chet Booth.

"Jesus, I hate that prick."

Chrissy Cassidy shrugged. "Join the crowd."

\*\*\*

Jordan met Chet in the parking lot next to United Exceptionalism. Chet was wearing a polo shirt and khakis and had a duffel bag with him. As Jordan approached, Chet squinted, appraising the amateur journalist. He reached down into his bag and withdraw a baseball hat, which he immediately put on sideways.

"Your hat's a little crooked," Jordan said as he got to the car Chet was leaning against.

"Yeah, that's how I like to wear it."

They were standing beside a red Porsche, which Jordan assumed belonged to Chet, but he didn't care enough to ask.

"You ready to start?" he said instead.

"Sure."

"Why should people vote for you for senior class president?"

"I want to return the academy to its roots. I have a vision for United Exceptionalism that will return it to the type of institution the founders envisioned."

"What I mean is, why should anyone vote for you,

given how much you're disliked?"

"Oh." Chet blinked over and over. His eyes darted to his duffel bag as if something in there might save him. "Oh," he said again.

"You tried to get the school dance cancelled. You tried to get our field trip cancelled. Why would anyone vote for someone to be senior class president if he tries to ruin something every time he doesn't get his own way?"

For a moment, Chet went perfectly still. He didn't blink. When time resumed and he did speak again, all he said was, "Oh."

\*\*\*

This is how Jordan started his article about Chet:

*Four students are running for senior class president. While each of them has questions they'll need to answer, only Chet Booth will have to answer for trying to get both a school dance and a field trip cancelled. Why did Chet Booth oppose these popular events? Because he simply didn't like them, and when Chet Booth doesn't get his way, he tries to ruin it for everyone else.*

\*\*\*

This is how the piece about Chet began after Chrissy Cassidy reviewed it:

*Four students are running for senior class president. While each of them has questions they'll need to answer, only Chet Booth will have to answer for trying to get both a school dance and a field trip cancelled. Why did Chet Booth oppose these popular events? Because he simply didn't like them, and when Chet Booth doesn't get his way, he tries to ruin it for everyone else.*

# 14

Sara Davenport-Shrep wrote articles for *The Representative* because Brian Toppert also did. Of course, she didn't find out until after she signed up for the activity that Brian already had a crush on Hannah Morganson. Jordan Sustabal flirted with her but Jordan didn't have the same dimples that Brian had, and so she only returned the attention half-heartedly.

"Your assignment," Chrissy Cassidy said, "is to interview Reginald Cript."

"The rich kid?"

"That's the one."

"I thought he was joking about running for senior class president. He's actually serious?"

Chrissy sighed. Her patience with the sophomore reporter was already waning.

"Apparently so."

\*\*\*

Cript said he wasn't interested in meeting in the cafeteria or library or anywhere else at United Exceptionalism. If Sara wanted the privilege of interviewing him, she would have to go to his house to do so.

Her own home was quite nice, three stories, brick, built in 1910. It had a long driveway lined with trees on either side, a large pool in the backyard, and a staircase on either side of the house.

Cript's house, though, or rather his parents' house, was unlike anything she had seen before. She had heard stories of it from kids who had attended Cript's parties but she had never been deemed popular enough to be invited. A large iron fence, painted gold, surrounded the entire twenty-acre estate. The pair of guesthouses combined to equal the size of her entire house. Cript's primary home, a white mansion set between the two guesthouses, looked like a historic hospital or bank headquarters or some other institution meant for hundreds of people. The backyard reportedly had two tennis courts, an indoor basketball court, an Olympic-sized swimming pool, a shooting range, and even a go-cart racetrack. Some of the students of United Exceptionalism were said to race there and drink beer served by the Cripts' butler whenever Reginald's parents were away.

"Hello?" she said through her rolled down window at the intercom outside the gate.

The only response was the intercom buzzing and the regal gate opening. It was said that the Cripts' driveway was so long the state had made Reginald's father conform to a county ordinance by putting up a speed limit sign just inside their property. It was also said that this requirement annoyed the Cripts—who didn't think the local government had any right telling them what they could and couldn't do on their own property—so much that they intentionally goaded the town into taking them to court. Once there, Mr. Cript's lawyers cost the town a fortune. Cript eventually lost, but ultimately cost the town millions in taxpayer dollars to argue about a sign on private property. When the local paper mentioned how much the trial cost, the judge and lead prosecutor both faced so much pressure that they had to step down. Once the sign was up, Cript had his gardener plant a tall bush directly in front of it so it was obstructed. Knowing Cript was daring the county to waste more money in legal fees, the authorities let the matter go.

On her way into the estate, Sara passed a tall bush on her right. She suspected it was there to block the sign she'd heard about, and it probably wasn't a coincidence that the small tree had been trimmed to resemble a hand giving the middle finger.

*\*\*\**

"Can I get you anything?" Reginald asked. "Some orange juice? Some water?" He winked and added, "Maybe something to take the edge off?"

Sara was too overwhelmed by the house's entryway to pay him much attention. On the walls in front of her were several antique paintings, one depicting two ancient armies going into battle, another of boats sailing in turbulent waters, a landscape of rolling hills with an old cottage in the distance. The largest painting of all was a family portrait of Reginald standing in front of his parents. Each piece of art was surrounded in heavy gilded frames that themselves might each have been worth a small fortune.

Above the paintings hung a chandelier with thousands of finely cut crystals. Further down the hallway were framed photographs, most with two people standing side by side. They were too far away for her to see but she guessed they would be photos of Reginald's father with various celebrities and politicians.

Cript saw her eyes go toward the pictures of his father and grew impatient. "Well, are you here to interview me or stand on the rug?"

Her cheeks burned and her gaze dropped to her shoes.

"This way," Reginald said, pointing to a pair of white sofas near a wall that was almost entirely made of glass so anyone could look out and see all of the extravagant activities taking place in the backyard.

She sat on the nearer of the two sofas. For a moment, Cript hovered over her as if he intended to sit beside her instead of on the other sofa, and her face reddened a second time. At the last minute, close enough to smell her shampoo, Cript angled to the side and sat on the other sofa.

Sara was still getting her pad of paper and pencil out of her bag when Reginald said, "I haven't got all day. What's the first question?"

Still gathering her materials, she clicked RECORD on her cell phone in case she missed anything and asked the first question from memory. "Why are you running for senior class president?"

This question, for some reason, made him smile and wink at her.

"I want to make the academy great again. It used to be a really fine place. My dad talks about what it was like back when he attended. Now, you have girls walking around in jeans and dresses. If you ask me, girls who wear that stuff instead of skirts and nice uniforms are all sluts. Sure, some of them may be nice girls. I wouldn't mind hooking up with some of them myself, but if they're going to dress that way they should go to another academy."

The lead point of Sara's pencil was stuck on the paper, refusing to budge. She'd heard what Reginald had just said, but her brain had difficulty processing it.

"Wait, girls who wear jeans are sluts? You can't be serious."

Cript's eyes went to Sara's legs. They were covered in denim. For a third time, her cheeks felt like they were on fire.

"I'm definitely serious, sweetheart. Listen, I know girls. My father employs a ton of them. The ones you got to look out for are wearing jeans or dresses. I've never seen a girl wear a nice skirt who was trouble."

As the words sank in, the preposterousness of them made Sara snort with laughter.

Reginald's voice grew louder and all the joviality in his face vanished. "What's so fucking funny?"

"I know plenty of girls who wear jeans. I know a bunch who wear dresses. None of them are sluts. I don't know where you get your info, but you might want to check again."

"Listen, girly"—he was standing up now—"I know women. I was dating girls a hundred times hotter than you when you were still reading Harry Potter with your loser friends."

As he began to walk away, she said, "Hey, where are you going? Are we done?"

He smiled and pointed to the front door. "Yeah, I'm finished. You know what, girly? Why don't you go back and play some more Dungeons and Dragons with your friends or whatever else it is you do because you have to be better at that than you are at interviewing people." He paused, considering something. "Oh, and if *The Representative* ever wants to do another piece on me, have them send someone else next time. You're blacklisted."

\*\*\*

This is how Sara's article began:

*"If you ask me, girls who wear that stuff (jeans and dresses) instead of skirts and nice uniforms are all sluts." That's how Reginald Cript feels about a large segment of the student body at United Exceptionalism. Cript, who is running to become the Traditionalist candidate for senior class president, says this in the hope it will convince you to vote for him later this year.*

\*\*\*

This is how the article appeared when it was posted online:

*"If you ask me, girls who wear that stuff (jeans and dresses) instead of skirts and nice uniforms are all sluts." That's how Reginald Cript feels about a large segment of the student body at United Exceptionalism. Cript, who is running to become the Traditionalist candidate for senior class president, says this in the hope it will convince you to vote for him later this year.*

# 15

Because of how much power the senior class president held at United Exceptionalism, the academy did something different than most other schools. The entire student body, even freshmen, participated in selecting the next senior class president. This gave each student a voice in who would make the important decisions that would affect the school for the next year.

The day after *The Representative* posted their interviews of the candidates, a group of freshmen boys, each with a different comic book character on their T-shirt, sat at a lunch table next to a group of senior girls, each of whom played on their cell phones more than they spoke to each other.

"It seems real obvious," a boy with a Batman shirt said. "Shelly McMarton's the clear choice."

A boy with a West Coast Avengers T-shirt nodded and said, "None of the others have any experience. Like, zero. Shelly's entire life has gotten her ready to become senior class president."

None of the boys questioned if that might actually be something to take pity on her for.

The senior girl closest to the boys' table, who had to try the hardest to act as if the nerds didn't exist, said, "Spend two seconds around that twat and tell me if you trust a single word she says."

Another girl chimed in, "Whatever she says, believe the exact opposite." Then, nudging the girl next to her, she added, "Like Billy said, 'Just the tip', right?" then burst into a frenzy of laughter while the other girl sulked.

"Why would *The Representative* lie?" a boy asked as he strategically placed his peanut butter and jelly sandwich in front of Wolverine's face to obscure it from the popular girls who were actually talking to him.

The leader of the girls let the corners of her mouth curl with disdain. "It's what they do, kid."

At the far end of the table, a girl with sunglasses on top of her head despite spending the entire day indoors, said, "I get what you're saying: Shelly's a devious motherfucker. But what's the alternative? Percy Wethers? If he actually thinks he could do any of the things he talks about, I want some of what he's smoking."

None of the girl's friends knew she only said that because her parents promised she could go to Burning Man the following year if she helped say and do whatever it took to get Shelly elected.

***

After school, the wide receivers were out on the football field, taking turns catching passes from a machine that spit out footballs in perfect spirals.

"I swear, if my dead grandma and Shelly were in a room and you forced me to see one of them naked, I'd pick my dead grandma."

The other boys laughed. The machine ejected another football and a tall, lanky senior caught it in the very middle of a diamond he formed with the thumb and index finger of his hands.

Another of the receivers said, "Janet Paelianio cheated on me with her ex, promised it would never happen again, then cheated on me again, and I still believe her more than anything that comes out of McMarton's mouth."

"Has she said what her stance is on the dress code yet?"

"Just ask the alumni what they want. That'll be her stance."

The shortest of the receivers was a kid named Chip Quintano. Chip warmed the bench during games. His role was to pass water bottles to the kids who actually played. None of his teammates knew his father had promised to buy him a new roadster if he helped get Shelly elected.

"She is pretty awful," Chip said. "But who else is there? Chet Booth is a complete sack of shit. Reginald Cript sounds insane. The only other choice is that Percy Wethers kid we've barely heard of before he started offering free stuff to everyone. I'll take my chances with Shelly if those are the options."

***

The following day, in the very middle of the cafeteria, a group of sophomore boys, each of whom wished they were already seniors, flirted with a table full of freshman girls. To adolescent boys, anything could and would be turned into a sexual innuendo. And all of it was hilarious only to them.

The girls ignored all of this. What they cared about much more was what Percy Wethers had been saying. Supposedly, if they voted for him, they'd be allowed to wear flip-flops the following year. Not just that, they'd also get free laptops to use in class. They also heard their textbooks would be a fraction of what they currently cost, which would make their parents happy.

Their other choices were a lying and conniving girl who cared nothing about the students, a goon who looked like a scarecrow had come to life with a creepy smile plastered on his face, or a sexist and privileged jerk. The choice seemed clear enough.

***

Even though *The Representative* dismissed Percy as having lofty and unrealistic goals, the freshman and sophomores at United Exceptionalism flocked to hear what he had to say. Most of the students either had no idea who Percy was and tagged along with their friends, or else wanted an excuse to eat lunch where all the freshman girls were going. That place was the smaller of the academy's two gymnasiums.

They met there because it had enough room for the kids to sit and eat while they listened to Percy speak. The gym talks started spontaneously; a table full of sophomores had overheard what Percy was saying to some freshmen and wanted to hear it for themselves. Another table of freshmen saw that group of kids leaving en masse and wanted to know what was going on. Before long, the best place to hear Percy speak was the gym.

None of those in attendance had been students at the academy back when Jorge M. Shrub sent the football team off to Iroquois Regional High School or when he ignored the flooded classroom, but they had heard the horror stories. They also heard, because word of mouth among high schoolers spread faster than anything *The Representative* could post, that Shelly wasn't to be trusted. Not only that, some of the kids said she had actually been in favor of many of the things Shrub had done and was known to constantly change her stance according to who she was speaking with. But worse than all of that, she had a reputation for caring more about what the alumni wanted than the students around her.

Day after day, more and more kids went to the gymnasium. While Shelly's faculty advisor was speaking to a reporter from *The Representative* and Shelly was talking to two teachers who were clearly only humoring her and wanted to get away, Percy Wethers was speaking to a room full of cheering kids. While Chet Booth was begging anyone to listen to how he would return the school to the vision its founders had and Reginald Cript was either denying what he had said about girls who wore jeans or else was bragging about his supposed escapades, the underclassmen gathered in the gym to hear a junior with moppy hair and ill-fitting clothes talk about flip-flops and free laptops.

***

Anna and Yeri were also in attendance during the earliest gymnasium talks. They'd been holding hands after finishing their lunches and saw a group of students follow Percy out of the cafeteria. With nothing better to do, they followed.

The couple whispered to each other while Percy transformed himself from shy and awkward boy to loud and energetic public speaker.

"My mom said Percy will never win," Anna said.

"My dad said the same thing. He says it'll be McMarton versus Cript in the second round."

Anna brought her hands up to her opposite shoulders, feigning a shiver. "Can you imagine how awful that would be?"

As she spoke, Percy got to another of his talking points and all of the kids around her broke into applause at what they were hearing.

# 16

Chet Booth sat with other kids at lunch as well. However, they weren't his friends. They were other social outcasts. Across from him sat Max Schisinger and Gay McDermott. Max was a senior at United Exceptionalism and was best known for getting an erection during music class in fifth grade. Somehow, Max hadn't understood what was happening or that there could be a social stigma to doing what he did next, which was to announce his erection to the rest of his classmates. Not only that, he showed it to them. Poor Max had never lived the moment down. He had one more year of torture before he could go to a college where no one knew him and begin a second life as *Max Schisinger the Ordinary Kid* rather than *Mad Max the Boner Flasher.*

Even some of the kids who made fun of Gay McDermott felt bad about it. It was actually Gay's parents who deserved the ridicule rather than their son. Odd last names could be forgiven. Brett Fahrt was relentlessly called Brett the Stink Fart. Tommy Titch was known as Tommy Tit. But even the kids who yelled these nicknames knew they were juvenile. But Gay McDermott's first name had been entirely within his parents' control and they had still picked it over any other.

It was rumored that Gay was going to legally change his name as soon as he graduated from United Exceptionalism.

Max and Gay were the only two kids who allowed Chet Booth to sit with them. None of three boys spoke to one another.

\*\*\*

On the other side of the cafeteria, a pair of junior boys waited in line to buy a cup of ice cream.

"Did you see what *The Representative* had to say about Booth?"

The other boy laughed. "They actually went easy on him. He's such an asshole that literal assholes would be afraid to get shit on them if they got too close."

"It's almost like the guy doesn't realize how much people hate him."

\*\*\*

In the gymnasium, Anna and Yeri were listening to Percy Wethers while simultaneously looking at pictures on their cell phones. One showed an image of the clown from Stephen King's It with the caption "Not as creepy as Chet Booth." There were a dozen other pictures just like it.

# 17

A third of the academy identified as Reformist, and so they immediately argued that anything Reginald Cript said about girls in jeans was sexist nonsense. Of the other two thirds of the students, feelings were mixed. Understandably, most girls were offended. But many of the boys thought it was funny. None of them would have come out and said something as outrageous as Cript. The fact that Cript *had* said it out loud, and not only that, but that he had offered it as a reason everyone at United Exceptionalism should vote for him, was so funny that the immature part of them flocked to see what Reginald might say next.

Yes, the academy was supposed to be preparing its students for the next step in their education, and yes, they all came from affluent if not disgustingly wealthy families, but a kid saying dumb stuff for laughs would always play to the base instincts of teenagers. After all, these were boys who would say or do anything it took to get laid. They were kids who made sure they were a safe distance away from someone else's fart, then laughed along with everyone else at the noise it had made.

\*\*\*

There was also a segment of the student body, while significantly smaller than the immature group, who actually liked what Cript said. These were the boys who knew at least one girl who wore jeans and who actually was promiscuous. In their minds, if the one slutty girl they knew did wear jeans, maybe Cript was onto something.

They would never admit to feeling that way, especially not in a public place like the halls or cafeteria of United Exceptionalism. They certainly wouldn't announce a feeling like that to the entire academy. In their eyes, the fact that Cript had said that exact thing didn't just make him the best choice for senior class president, it made him a hero.

\*\*\*

Last of all, the smallest group of boys who approved of what Cript said: those who resented girls. Not for any good reason, but because they had been turned down by one and the rejection had stung them to their core.

Bill Bojama had asked Amy McCluster out three different times. Each occasion, she had said no. Amy wore jeans. The fact that she wasn't interested in Bill or in dating in general and definitely wasn't a slut was beside the point. What was important was that when Cript called out girls like Amy, they were embarrassed the same way Bill had been embarrassed. Reginald Cript was punishing girls like Amy for not dating boys like Bill and that was all the more reason to like him.

\*\*\*

The very first argument Anna and Yeri ever had was about liking Cript. Yeri didn't like him, he detested the kid, but one of his friends thought Cript was great.

"How can you be friends with him?" Anna said, her face contorted with concern.

"What? I'm going to not be friends with someone

just because they like Reginald Cript and I don't? That's ridiculous."

"So now I'm being ridiculous?"

"That's not what I said. I'm just saying, I don't like him but if Reggie likes him, that's Reggie's prerogative."

"You're supporting him by property of transference!"

"Okay, *now* you're being ridiculous!"

He leaned in to give her a kiss to let her know he was joking, but she turned away. She gave him the silent treatment the rest of the day. When they arrived at United Exceptionalism the next morning, they were a happy couple again.

# 18

Mr. Podulski barely had a chance to look up from the quizzes he was grading when Shelly stormed into his classroom, slamming the door behind her.

"What the fuck?" she shrieked.

In a short amount of time, she had gotten very comfortable cursing like a sailor in her faculty advisor's company. It was one of the only ways she felt like she was getting his full attention.

"Calm down," he said.

The red pen in his hand drew a line through a student's answer and then scribbled the correct answer.

"Calm down? Do you even know why I'm here?"

He looked up from the quiz. "Please, do tell."

"He's getting more popular every day. The kids love him. They fucking love him. If they could, they'd have, like, ten thousand of his goddamned babies. Flip-flops at school? Are you kidding me? Free laptops? That's the dumbest fucking thing I've ever heard."

She was almost screaming by the time she finished. Mr. Podulski didn't need to be told who Shelly was talking about.

"It'll be fine." His eyes went back to grading the quiz. "I have it taken care of."

"You have it taken care of?" She snorted with derision and tapped a foot against the tile floor. "You have it under control? That piece of shit is becoming a legend. Do you know how many kids are going to the gymnasium to hear him talk about the damn dress code and cheaper textbooks?"

Mr. Podulski rolled his eyes, not at Shelly, but at a wrong answer on the quiz in front of him.

"He says things they want to hear," the teacher said.

Shelly's eyes bulged. "No shit. No fucking sh—"

She stopped when the Economics teacher glanced up from his desk and gave her a look that told her she was overstepping her bounds.

"I'm sorry," she said. "It's just that, well, I can't compete with that. I can't get hundreds of kids to come hear me talk. I can't get them to cheer after I say something."

"I know," Mr. Podulski said, his voice soothing. "And you don't have to. Just keep doing what you're doing and everything will be fine."

"I'm not doing anything."

The slightest of grins came over his face. "Precisely. Keep doing that and my helpers will do everything else." When she started to offer a complaint, his speech quickened and any patience he had exhibited was gone. "It's what you have to do. The kids don't like you. The less they see or hear of you, the better." Then, smiling again, as if he were both the bad cop and the good cop, he winked and added, "Let the machine go into action. We'll win it for you."

***

Melissa and Rachel were two of the only students at United Exceptionalism who were friends and knew what the other person was up to: both were working to get Shelly elected. Melissa was getting paid twenty-five dollars an hour by her father for her efforts. After coming home drunk the previous weekend, Rachel was doing it so she would only be grounded one week instead of one month.

The two girls didn't have to canvass neighborhoods (which they wouldn't have been caught doing anyway) or write articles for *The Representative* or attend speeches given by Shelly. All they had to do was sit in Melissa's bedroom and take turns posting things on the internet.

They started by making a list of websites where students from United Exceptionalism met online. This was mainly the school's Facebook group, but also the discussion board on *The Representative* and a few other sites. Where they were allowed to post anonymously, they did. Where they had to have a real name, they created a fake account under a freshman's name and posted under that.

For the next couple of hours, they took turns posting as much good stuff about Shelly as they could think of and as much negative stuff about Percy as they could dream up. Only five or six other kids were posting to the same websites while Melissa and Rachel did their dirty work. Because the two girls shared a variety of fictitious accounts, it looked like half of the discussion was based on the notion that Shelly McMarton was the only reasonable choice for senior class president and that Percy Wethers was an awkward wacko who lived in a dream world. It wasn't long before every site was plastered with messages from what appeared to be a large segment of the

75

school but which was actually two girls sharing a single computer.

\*\*\*

Chrissy Cassidy, editor of *The Representative*, didn't know which other students were working to help get Shelly elected, but she knew they were out there. When she saw the slew of comments on United Exceptionalism's Facebook group about how awful Percy Wethers was and how great Shelly McMarton would be, she knew what was going on.

It didn't matter to her that the negative posts couldn't be verified as actual students. She read a couple comments about how kids were supposedly growing tired of hearing Percy say the same things about flip-flops and free laptops and were beginning to doubt if he had anything else of substance to talk about.

She immediately began to write the next article.

*Go on any United Exceptionalism website these days and you'll read the same thing: students are concerned that Percy Wethers has nothing but empty promises to offer and are coming to the realization that Shelly McMarton has the experience and demeanor necessary to lead United Exceptionalism...*

\*\*\*

"We need something catchy," Rachel said, popping her chewing gum and playing on her smartphone.

Melissa paused from posting another fictitious student's complaint on Facebook and looked around her room for inspiration. Various boy band posters were on the walls. A bunch of dirty clothes were sitting in a corner.

"I've got it! I was at lunch the other day and this girl called him a perv."

"Okay," Rachel said, her tone skeptical.

"Percy's Pervs! Anyone who supports the perv is also a perv."

Even as Melissa said she loved it, she was already posting the next comment on Facebook.

\*\*\*

Chrissy set a lofty goal for herself—one negative story about Percy every hour for an entire day. After reading the latest Facebook post, the next article basically wrote itself.

*A troubling new phenomenon has come to light during Percy Wethers's run for senior class president. The moniker "Percy's Pervs" has become popular online to note the immature boys who only support Percy because they want to see just how relaxed he'll make the dress code, all in hopes of catching a glimpse of the female portion of the student body. These "Percy's Pervs," as they've become known, are a black mark on the reputation of United Exceptionalism, and anyone openly supporting Percy should question their motives...*

\*\*\*

Melissa and Rachel were going at full steam now. The only thing slowing them down was the need to switch back and forth between different fake accounts.

"Post something about how it's sexist of Percy's Pervs to support him. Hell, post that it's sexist of Percy to run in the first place because everyone should support Shelly."

Rachel gave her friend a skeptical look.

"Post it!"

Rachel grinned and began to type another message.

\*\*\*

77

The next morning, Chrissy had another editorial comment:

*The world has a long and well-documented history of holding women back, of sexism prevailing in every aspect of society. It even impacts us here at United Exceptionalism. It's widely understood that Shelly is the most experienced and qualified candidate to run for senior class president. It's clearly her time to lead the academy. Why then, would Percy take the attention away from her? Why would his group of Pervs rally around him other than because they're sexist? Can Percy prove he isn't sexist?...*

# 19

Everyone was whispering when school started the next Monday. Percy was a pervert and was sexist, and not only that, so were all of the students who liked him.

"Does that make me a perv?" Yeri asked. "Because I think the kid makes sense?"

"Does that make me sexist?" Anna replied. "Because I'd rather vote for him than some girl simply because she's a girl? What kind of argument is that to make?"

Up and down the hallways, other couples, friends, and even teachers, were in small groups, discussing the articles that had been written about McMarton and Wethers.

Yeri said, "I don't think they realize how awful of an argument that is: vote for me because it's sexist not to. How could anyone expect to win that way?"

Anna nodded. "What I don't get is that Shelly still refuses to say what she stands for. That's the best way to get more people excited for her and she refuses to do it."

Reginald Cript was walking past as Anna said this. He looked back over his shoulder as he continued walking down the hallway and said, "If your boyfriend introduced himself telling you he was going to fuck you, you wouldn't have gone out with him. But he probably sat quietly on the first date and the second date and kept doing that until he got in your pants. That's what McMarton is doing." He was almost shouting now because he was so far down the hallway. "Give her a chance, though, and she'll fuck you." Then, right before he disappeared around the corner, added, "That's why you should vote Cript!"

*\*\*\**

What Percy hoped was that none, or at least very few, of the students would care about what was posted on *The Representative* or in Facebook discussions. What they should care about was what they actually saw with their own eyes. And what they saw was one person running as the Reformist candidate for senior class president who never committed to what she supposedly believed while the other candidate yelled his ideas from the gymnasium floor. One had ever-changing values and the other had believed in the same policies his entire time at United Exceptionalism. To Percy, it was an easy choice.

*\*\*\**

Percy only met with his faculty advisor once a week. Ms. Wells was a Social Sciences teacher in her sixties who earned valuable street cred with her students for having been a genuine hippie when she was their age. The way she spoke, the gentle mannerisms with her hands, gave the impression that some part of her would always be a hippie.

They rarely met because Percy's strategy was simple: go out and talk to as many students as he could find; the more kids who heard what he had to say, the more would vote for him.

This time, though, they did need to discuss an important issue. Not the things that had been posted about him. Rather, the teacher's influence on the voting. Elections for senior class president were run differently at United Exceptionalism than at other schools. Each of the fifty classrooms voted for a candidate, but the teacher of each classroom also voted, and the teacher's vote carried a lot of weight.

"It's a way," Ms. Wells said, "to ensure kids such as yourself don't get elected, that the academy has some form of control in who becomes senior class president. Because of this, you're already behind in the voting."

Percy frowned. "But no one's even voted yet."

Ms. Wells' voice grew somber, the tone she either used when coming down off a high or when security guards confiscated joints at a good concert. "Trust me, you're already behind in the voting."

"Then I just need to get an even larger portion of the students' votes."

"That's another issue."

Percy knew which topic was going to come up next: homerooms. At United Exceptionalism, each student who ran for senior class president could generally count on his own homeroom to vote for him or her. It didn't happen every time, but it happened most times. The problem was that he only had one homeroom and it was one that didn't have many students in it.

"Your opponent says she has three different homerooms. Supposedly, she's from everywhere."

\*\*\*

The crowd in the gymnasium that day was the largest one yet. Never before had a senior class president candidate's rally drawn more than a few dozen students, let alone nearly two hundred of them. Now, in addition to the freshman and sophomores, some upper classmen were there.

"You know what pains me?" Percy Wethers bellowed. "All around this gym I see kids who just want to go to a nice school, be happy, and go on to do better things in this world. Why is that too much to ask for?"

The first murmurs of approval and applause began to rise from the audience.

"I look around the gym and I don't see anyone who actually wants to go to Iroquois High School and beat up the kids there. You have more important things to worry about, don't you?"

The applause grew louder.

"It was a great tragedy for this academy to send the football team to that school. It'll go down as one of the greatest blunders this institution has ever faced. It also shows we need a change in the type of senior class president that runs this academy."

A girl stood up and yelled, "I love you, Percy."

A boy held up a sign that read, "Percy talks *about* flip-flops. Shelly *actually* flip-flops."

He told them that they shouldn't vote for anyone who supported the decisions Jorge M. Shrub made two years earlier and they applauded and cheered. He told them that the only reason textbooks cost so much was because a couple of wealthy alumni were getting rich off the students by marking up the books before selling them to the academy. They cheered even louder. He told them they shouldn't have to ask their parents or anyone else to buy them a laptop in order to learn, that the academy should provide them with brand new laptops if they cared about the students. They cheered for this loudest of all.

# 20

Chet Booth was having a tough go. No one wanted to hear him speak about what he could do as senior class president, or anything else, for that matter. He stood in the middle of the cafeteria and began delivering a strident speech about the esteemed history of the academy and the importance of preserving its founding principles. The students at the tables closest to Chet ignored him as long as they could. When they were unable to endure him any longer, a senior tossed his half-empty milk carton, hitting Booth in the face and spraying him with room-temperature milk.

He dried off and went to another table to sit down with a half dozen freshman girls. Before he could say anything, one of them told him to get bent. The others all laughed hysterically, picked up their trays, and left.

\*\*\*

Later, Chet stopped by the office of *The Representative* and knocked on the open door. The paper's editor looked up from the computer where she was typing.

"What?" she said, her eyes already back to her screen.

"I was hoping you'd be interested in doing a story on me, maybe help me get my ideas out to the school."

"No, thanks."

\*\*\*

Desperate to seem well-liked and painfully aware he was running out of time, Chet resorted to a new tactic: he recruited his family. The next day, his younger sister, a freshman at United Exceptionalism, was walking down the halls with a group of girls. Chet knew that none of the girls wanted to talk to him, but because he was the older brother of Suzie Booth, they would at least tolerate him. Meanwhile, all the other kids in the hall would see that a group of popular underclass girls liked hanging out with him. To Chet, it was a maneuver that would one day be included in his memoirs.

"Hey, sis," he said, a big smile stretched across his face.

Immediately, though, he realized his plan wasn't going to unfold the way he thought it would. Instead of saying hello in return, his sister blushed and put her head down. There was no way he could turn around and act like he hadn't said hello; he had spoken too loudly to pretend it hadn't happened and walk away.

"Hey, sis," he said again, the genuine delight in his smile giving way to a strained expression pasted over his genuine panic.

Instead of acknowledging him, Suzie actually turned her back to him while the other girls in the group laughed. His little sister's face was so red that it spread to the sides of her neck. He was fully committed, though. She had to understand that. Why was she doing this to him during such an important time in his life?

He tried to put his arm around her but she slunk away. His sister's friends were laughing hysterically now. He saw a glimpse of his sister's face as he came up beside her a second time for another try at putting his arm around her. When he did, he saw she was near tears. Without any other option, he forced his arm around her, smiled at all of her friends, kissed his sister on the cheek, and then left the scene as fast as he could without getting in trouble for running in the hallways.

*** 

An article in *The Representative* was posted hours

later. It featured a photograph that one of Suzie's friends had taken. The picture clearly showed Chet trying to force his arm around his sister's shoulder while she cried. The headline read:

*Sister of Anti-Dance Candidate Can't Stand Him Either*

# 21

Unlike Chet Booth, who seemed to only appear in *The Representative* when his sister rebuffed him, Reginald Cript couldn't stay out of its headlines. Everything he said and did became a sensation that was immediately posted to Facebook, Twitter, and everywhere else.

Most of the time, regardless of what he said and how *The Representative* covered it, Cript only became more popular. After starting his campaign with the brash statement that girls who wore jeans were sluts, he realized he could say anything he wanted and get away with it. He expanded on that provocative stance by saying that if girls who wore jeans insisted on attending classes at United Exceptionalism, they should have to sit in the corner and have screens put around them to block them from the rest of the class. He also claimed to have not only dated but bedded some of the most popular girls at school.

"They love my money. They couldn't resist. And I couldn't resist them." He said this last part with a grin that was meant to convey that a true gentleman didn't kiss and tell, only insinuated.

These girls all denied having had anything to do with Cript. It didn't matter, though. Once he said it, half the academy believed it and even many of the students who didn't believe it admired him for having the nerve to say something so outrageous.

Other times, he would mention a celebrity or world leader and say he had met them and that the two of them were friendly. No one at *The Representative* was able to reach these people to confirm the validity of the claims, so once again, half the academy thought of Reginald as a jet-setting friend to the elite.

***

At lunch, students from each grade would approach Cript and ask for selfies with him. He was always happy to oblige because it was another chance for his face to appear online.

"What you said about girls who wear jeans being sluts…" a senior named Tommy said.

Cript braced himself for one of two reactions. Either the kid would give him a high-five or else he would threaten to beat the shit out of him.

Tommy looked around to see how many people were listening, then leaned in and said, "I dated Jenny Milkchen and she cheated on me with half the school. And you know what? She wears jeans!"

A smile washed over Cript's face and his shoulders relaxed.

"That's what I'm saying. So I can count on your support?"

"Totally!"

***

Day after day, kids asked Reginald questions just so he had the opportunity to say something funny. Walking by a table full of junior girls, one asked what Cript thought of Chet Booth.

"Ugly Chet? Well, honestly, I don't think you should be eligible to be senior class president if you look like the Elephant Man."

The girls laughed and went back to eating their lunch.

He passed a table of freshman boys who asked what he thought about Shelly McMarton.

"Desperate Shelly? She's the one girl who could wear jeans and no one—no one!—would think she was a slut. Seriously, who would want to come within a hundred yards of touching that monster? She should have her own dress code. What are trolls and gremlins supposed to wear? Whatever it is, that's what she should be wearing."

One boy sprayed water out through his nose. Another coughed up the piece of apple he'd been eating. All of them applauded Cript as he made his way through the lunchroom.

# 22

When Shelly McMarton arrived at school the next day, there were flyers everywhere. Most had a picture of Percy Wethers's face or a caricature exaggerating his uncombed hair and lanky frame. Under one was the caption "Flip-flops, Free Laptops, and a Bankrupt Academy." Another had Percy dressed as Santa Claus with the caption "Every Day Is Christmas When Percy Gives Away Free Stuff." Another had his face put on Stalin's body and the caption, "This Is How It Begins."

Each flyer made her laugh more than the previous one.

\*\*\*

Anna and Yeri saw them too; the flyers were impossible to miss.

"I guess if you attract this kind of attention it means you're doing something right?" Yeri said, not sounding at all convinced.

"You're forgetting something."

"What's that?"

Anna reached up, took one of the flyers off the wall, crumpled it, then said, "Cript is also getting a lot of attention and he's certainly not doing anything right. The average kid is going to see this nonsense and believe it."

"Oh."

***

The odd thing was that for the most part, the endless stream of articles in *The Representative* about Percy Wethers and all the negative flyers plastered to the walls of the academy had the opposite effect of what was intended. Rather than shame Wethers, they seemed to increase his popularity. Freshmen took the flyers off the walls and posted them on their lockers as a way of showing their support.

Shelly McMarton saw a boy do this and grabbed him by the collar.

"Are you an idiot?" she asked.

"Everyone's tired of the same type of people running for senior class president," he replied. "Whoever put these signs up is reminding us that the alumni and faculty are afraid of Percy and want to keep things the way they are. That's why we love him."

She gritted her teeth. "Oh my god," she said. "You are an idiot."

***

Shelly paused in the hallway that led past the gymnasium that also acted as one of the academy's auditoriums. She wanted to get to the classroom at the other end of the hallway, but to do so she would either have to take the long way around or walk right past the main entrance to the gym. Normally, she wouldn't care. It was lunchtime, though, and Percy was giving another of his speeches to a packed auditorium of students who ate up everything he said.

She didn't dare show her face. In general, the other students were beneath her. But seeing crowds of underclassmen cheering for that buffoon drove her insane. The main thing she didn't want, though, was to be drawn into a situation where she was put on the spot. If she was forced to give her stance on a topic, any topic, it could be used against her. It took talent and cunning to remain free of any commitment on any issue.

"Hey, it's Shelly!"

Her awareness snapped back from her daydream in time to see the skinny kid who was watching her duck back into the gymnasium and shout that Shelly McMarton was in the hallway.

Her heart raced. Her eyes darted for the nearest escape route. Before she could run for cover, a dozen students were filing out into the hallway, all of them shouting for her to come into the gymnasium.

She couldn't act as though she hadn't heard them and simply walk away. Or could she? It was an enticing possibility but, before she could give it a shot and see what happened, ten more kids filed out of the gym and also called for her to join them. It was only when one of them raised a cell phone and took a photo of Shelly standing at the end of the hallway by herself—proof that it had happened, evidence she couldn't deny—that she grudgingly put one foot in front of the other and began toward the noise.

After two steps, one of the kids turned and shouted into the gymnasium, "She's coming! Shelly's coming!"

The kids cheered like maniacs. No amount of

delusion could trick her into believing they were happy to see her. It was the opposite; they wanted her to look like a fool. Well, she wasn't going to give them the pleasure. By the time she entered the auditorium, her chin was in the air and her eyes were blazing.

A few pennants hung from the rafters. One was from two decades earlier when the track and field team had won the state championship. Another, from the same timeframe, commemorated the boy's basketball team reaching the state finals. A pair of banners for the girl's soccer team noted they had won the state championship two years in a row.

Most of the bleachers were pulled out, with students from every grade taking up space on them. The bleachers came to within feet of the edge of the basketball court. The basketball hoops, rather than being in position for a game, had been drawn back toward the ceiling.

"Hi everyone," she shouted as she entered the room, a toothy smile on her face.

She was struck by the stench of sweat and body odor that pervaded the gym at all times. She was such a consummate professional, however, that the plastic smile plastered on her face didn't even flicker.

Percy stood by himself on a stage positioned at the far end of the gym. He waved to her and then motioned for her to join him. Even this made his pack of supporters cheer, and it took all of her willpower not to scream at them and ask what the hell they were so happy about.

Once she was at the stage, Percy, who no one had even heard of at the beginning of the school year, raised his hands for silence and the crowd complied.

"It's great to see you, Shelly. Thanks for coming."

As if she had a choice.

"It's great to be here," she said. "What a crowd you have."

From the bleachers, one kid yelled, "If you

become senior class president, am I gonna be able to wear my flip-flops?"

Another yelled, "Why don't you agree with Percy that we deserve free laptops?"

To both questions, half the audience clapped at the questions and the other half jeered at Shelly, assuming they weren't going to like whatever she said. No doubt Percy had already repeated his monologue for the thousandth time about the utopian fantasy world he could create for them.

She turned to the crowd, her smile showing off her white teeth. Even before she started to speak, a boy yelled, "Liar!" but she ignored it.

"Thanks for inviting me here," she began. "I've been looking forward to having a chance to share my views with all of you. The first thing I want to say is that I'm absolutely in favor of expanding the casual nature of the dress code. If you want to wear flip-flops, nobody should tell you that you can't."

The crowd was silent. Beside her, Percy coughed.

In the bleachers, Anna leaned over and whispered in Yeri's ear. "Yeah, right."

McMarton's voice grew in intensity when she said, "The truth is, I've been working behind the scenes to ensure that very thing happens. I've been reaching out to the current senior class president and to other key members of the student body to recommend that students be allowed to wear any type of clothing they want, regardless of color, style, or utility."

As she spoke, her hands generated more and more energy. It wasn't long before she looked like a wizard trying to cast a spell. No one could say she didn't look passionate about the right to wear flip-flops at school.

"And another thing," she said. "I wholeheartedly think that every student deserves a free laptop for use at United Exceptionalism, I just think there's a better way to go about providing them."

\*\*\*

*Today, The Representative was there when Shelly McMarton finally got a chance to share her ideas with the student body. Amongst the things they learned about her is that she has in fact been in favor of many of the same ideas Percy Wethers has been expounding upon, for even longer than her opponent. The difference is that instead of talking the talk, Shelly is walking the walk. While one candidate is working the students into a fervor with promises of free laptops, Shelly is the one actually working behind the scenes to make these things happen.*

*This brings up an important issue in the race: the issue of promises versus reality. Percy seems to be making a lot of empty promises that he has no way of actually implementing. Shelly, on the other hand, has a proven track record of working to improve the academy. When you look at it that way, there's only one reasonable option for senior class president: Shelly McMarton.*

# 23

A funny thing happened. Everywhere Percy went, students said he was the clear winner of the impromptu joint appearance with Shelly McMarton. Even the few kids who openly supported Shelly said she had reminded everyone in attendance why they didn't like her. Meanwhile, Percy had seemed like an average kid, which they liked.

The nearly unanimous praise wasn't enough for *The Representative* to take the same stance. The academy's newspaper insisted Shelly had won the informal debate. Yes, she could have shown more personality, the paper said, but she offered a firm message. And by simply not messing up, she had won.

"I don't understand," Anna said, reading the article on her smartphone as Yeri packed books into his backpack. "Percy didn't mess up either; he totally kicked her ass. But somehow, because Shelly didn't accidentally yell slurs or kill someone, she won?"

\*\*\*

An hour later, *The Representative* posted another story about the debate. This one praised Shelly for finally having a chance to convey her ideas, which, the editor said, provided the best parts of what Percy also proposed, but suggested it in a much more realistic fashion.

Every student who was actually in the gym and had seen what had happened knew one thing. The ones who relied on *The Representative* knew—or thought they knew—something completely different.

\*\*\*

"You can't be so nice."

That was what Percy's faculty advisor had told him after the debate in the gymnasium. It was the tenth time Ms. Wells had said it to him.

"They aren't wearing kid gloves for you, Percy. They're tearing you apart and you're just sitting there saying why the students should vote for you instead of telling them why they shouldn't vote for Shelly."

Thinking about that advice, Percy paced back and forth across the stage at the end of the gymnasium. It had gotten to the point where the kids in the audience started to clap before he spoke because they had heard him say all the same things countless times before.

"I don't want to win that way," he had told Ms. Wells, to which she could only sigh.

Time was running out, though. The first round of

voting to decide who would be the Reformist candidate and who would be the Traditionalist candidate was coming up soon. *The Representative* kept reminding everyone that, because of all the teachers who were going to be supporting Shelly, the race wasn't going to be close.

"Let me make this as clear for you as I can," he told the students gathered in the gym.

The kids in attendance immediately understood this wasn't going to be the normal speech Percy gave.

"You have two choices in front of you to be the Reformist candidate for senior class president. One supported Jorge M. Shrub sending the football team to beat up everyone at Iroquois Regional High School, sometimes says she's against expanding the dress code and sometimes says she's for it, and says free laptops aren't realistic but then says they might be. Would you rather have that person, who changes her stance depending on who she's talking to and who's supported the worst parts of this great academy's history, or would you have someone who's said the same things his entire time at United Exceptionalism?"

The kids, finally seeing Percy fight, cheered like they had never cheered before.

\*\*\*

The next day, a reporter from *The Representative* asked if she could interview Wethers again. Percy had no idea what type of questions the girl would ask but he gladly agreed. They met after school on the steps leading to the academy's main entrance.

"Thanks for agreeing to meet with me to answer some questions," the girl said.

She was a junior named Justine who supposedly wanted to be *The Representative*'s lead editor the following year. She put a pencil behind her ear before the interview started even though she typed all of Percy's responses into her laptop. It was apparent from the very first question that she didn't intend to write anything flattering or even neutral.

"Don't you think it's sexist to run against Shelly?"

He laughed at first. Then, when Justine's eyebrows rose and Wethers realized she was serious, he shook his head and sighed.

"Not at all. That question makes it sound as if she's somehow entitled to be the Reformist candidate for senior class president. Surely that's not what you're suggesting."

Justine jerked her head back so her hair wasn't in front of her eyes. After typing what seemed like much more than his simple response, she offered a smile.

"What about pointing out all the negative things she's said and done? Would you really be saying those things if Shelly were a boy?"

Percy couldn't help but blink in astonishment.

"Look at what Reginald Cript and Chet Booth are saying about each other. I never said anything personal. I merely pointed out what Shelly has actually supported and what she has actually said. How on earth could that possibly be considered sexist?"

Rather than answer, Justine went to her next question.

"She's the most qualified candidate. If she were senior class president, she would be the first female to hold that role since I've been at United Exceptionalism. Given those circumstances, you can see why people would say it seems like you're being unfair to her just because she's a girl."

Percy smiled and looked around for the masses of people to jump out and laugh at the prank they were playing. No one was there, though.

He said, "No one is saying that except for a couple of anonymous people online and a couple of writers at your paper. Do you know of anyone else at all who's expressed that idea?"

Justine squirmed against the marble step she was sitting on.

"Well," she said, "it's just that, you know, because of all the boys at the academy who call themselves Percy's Pervs. That seems sexist too, you know?"

He laughed, a genuine laugh, his head bobbing as he did so.

"No one calls themself a Percy's Perv. That's just another idea that was cooked up online and repeated in hopes that it sticks." He paused and shook his head. "Unless you can tell me of an actual instance of someone doing what you just said."

Instead of answering, Justine squinted at her notes, and Percy knew exactly what type of article was going to be posted about him in *The Representative*.

\*\*\*

"An odd thing happened today," Jerry Hedges said.

Jerry was one of Percy's oldest friends and one of the few kids who knew him before he started talking about flip-flops and free laptops.

Jerry said, "I was in the academy library and Ms. Wickers told me I wasn't going to be allowed to vote for senior class president unless I returned the book I checked out last month that's supposedly overdue. But that's the thing—I returned the book last week. Ms. Wickers says she can't find any record of it. I don't know what to do."

All Percy could do was laugh at the absurdity of it.

\*\*\*

Everywhere he went, throngs of students yelled his name and patted him on the back. Some told him it was great to see a normal kid running for senior class president for a change. Some said it was reassuring that he was there because he was the first person to actually have an ounce of common sense. Others liked that he cared more about what the students wanted than with satisfying the wishes of the alumni and faculty.

However, the teachers didn't see things the same way. Every teacher who spoke with *The Representative* said they were planning to vote for Shelly McMarton. Ms. Wells was right: the actual election hadn't even started yet and he was already losing.

# 24

Chet had never been well-liked, not since the school event shutdowns he almost caused. But the longer he tried to get his ideas across to students, the less they tolerated him. An air of resentment and irritation followed him everywhere he went.

When he told a group of freshman that he hoped they would vote for him, all of them called back, "Not even your own sister likes you."

It didn't help that he was sometimes seen wearing a leather coat near where the smokers hung out or a sideways baseball hat where the rebels congregated. No matter what he wore, no matter if he tried to sound like one of his classmates or if he tried to act like them, the students at United Exceptionalism weren't having any of it.

"Make sure you vote for me," he said to a pair of senior girls.

"Please die," the taller of the two girls said.

\*\*\*

His faculty advisor suggested that Chet might try and draw Reginald Cript into an argument in front of the other kids. It would be like the debate Percy had organized and that Shelly had clearly been dragged into against her will. The only difference would be that Chet wouldn't be as nice as Percy had been. As soon as Cript was in the same room with him, Chet would pounce, telling everyone that they should never vote for someone who degrades girls and who really hasn't stated any concrete actions for what he would do as senior class president.

With a new plan of attack, he approached a lunch table full of sophomores and said, "Wouldn't it be great if you got to hear Reginald and I compare our ideas?"

At first, all of them tried to ignore Chet and go on talking about some new game they had all downloaded to their phones.

It was only when he repeated himself that one of the boys rubbed his eyes and said, "Not really, man. None of us want to hear you talk. Not at all." And then, to seal the deal, the kid added, "No offense, dude. If it was anyone else, we'd love to hear them speak."

\*\*\*

Chet didn't give up, though. If he were the type of kid who quit in the face of adversity he never would have gone against the entire academy and opposed the school dance for trivial reasons.

He kept trying to get the kids interested in hearing him compare his ideas with Reginald's. He did this even though a football player emptied a yogurt container over his head. He did it even though his sister left the cafeteria any time she spotted him. And he did it even though Cript's new nickname for him—"Anus-Face Chet"—was catching on and being yelled at him wherever he went.

Finally, the persistence paid off. He was in the

middle of pleading with a group of senior girls when Reginald happened to walk by the same table.

"How about it, Reginald? Wanna meet up and see who the bigger man is?"

Chet couldn't help but smile. Cript's only option would be to accept.

Instead, Cript put his arm around one of the senior girls and smiled, then told the rest of the table, "Why would I ever do that? The only time anyone would ever want to hear Anus-Face Chet talk was if he was standing next to me. I wouldn't subject you lovely ladies to something that horrendous."

Then Reginald walked away and that was that.

# 25

*The Representative's* obsession with Reginald Cript was in full swing. Everything he said and did was front-page material at the expense of every other candidate, and each time a story was posted about him it was read by more students than stories about the football team, new after school activities, or anything else.

When asked if she would keep giving Cript a platform to spew his hate, Chrissy Cassidy said, "Of course. He's good for our readership numbers."

***

Cript told one reporter that maybe he wouldn't ban girls from being allowed to wear jeans because that would prevent him from getting to see a couple sweet asses. He then immediately voiced the concern that if he didn't ban jeans, he would be forced to see some of the dumpy asses more than he wanted.

"You can see the challenges I would face as senior class president," he said as he winked at the female reporter. "But I'm sure I'll figure it out once I'm elected."

***

Betsy Shonenberg-Newcastle was a freshman trying to make a name for herself at *The Representative*. She liked hanging around Chrissy Cassidy and the other upperclassmen and felt she could be a part of their club if she were a sophomore or junior. As a freshman, though, her options were limited. The only way to make herself known was by writing a better story about Cript than anyone else had written so far.

The article she wrote was published the following day. She called Cript "a small boy with loud ideas" who had "built an aura around himself embodying success at school, with women, and in life in general," but that all of it was a façade. "In reality," she wrote, "Many of his teachers, on condition of anonymity, said he was either failing or was barely passing their classes" and that "no girl would dare admit even going out on a date with Cript, let alone anything more serious."

She dissected the few stances he had put forth, calling them all juvenile and sexist. She cut through the persona of "Cript" that Reginald had created and painted a picture of an obsessed and timid boy who was afraid of not being liked.

For all of this, she paid a dear price.

***

Cript pulled into the parking lot in a black Maserati that the kids whispered was a loaner that Reginald's father never paid for. As soon as he got out of his car, he went looking for Betsy. He found her outside

99

the office of the academy newspaper, talking to a friend.

"Hey, you," he called to her from thirty yards away, causing everyone else to see who was yelling. "You're real special, you know that? I'm gonna start calling you Bitchy Betsy. How you like that?"

Betsy's face turned the color of a plum. Half the kids laughed at what they had heard. The other half didn't like Cript but they loved the spectacle of what was happening and so they stayed and watched as well.

"Bitchy Betsy," Reginald said. "I had no idea when you interviewed me that you were in the middle of having your period."

Her face twitched, her lip quivered. He was standing in front of her now but he didn't lower his voice.

"You're a real loser, you know that?" he said.

He stood over her so she either had to back away or else look up to see his chin above her forehead.

"Well, I'm gonna do you a favor, Bitchy Betsy. You're done. Next time your lousy paper wants to write a story about me, make sure it's not you or they won't get the interview. You're blacklisted. Hey, I'm doing you a favor; you have no talent so you're only wasting your time, Bitchy Betsy."

Even the kids who had started off laughing at Cript's antics were silent now, cringing at the train wreck they were seeing. Their lack of encouragement didn't deter Reginald, however. He kept going, yelling at Betsy in front of everyone until she rubbed at her eyes to keep the first tears from running down her face. Then she turned and ran into the office of *The Representative*, slamming the door behind her.

"Nice talking to you, Bitchy Betsy," Cript called from the other side of the door. Then, turning to the nearest set of students, smiled and said, "I think she took it personally."

# Winter Semester

# 1

Unlike the final election, the first round of voting for senior class president wasn't done in a single day. Instead, it was carried out over the entirety of the winter semester. The fifty classrooms voted one by one. On some days, one class would vote in the morning and another in the afternoon. Other days, only one class would vote. Some days, no votes were held at all.

Everyone agreed it would be simpler, quicker, and more cost effective to have the entire student body vote on the same day, as they did in the final round of voting. No one was sure why it was done this way instead.

When the process was over, there would be one Reformist candidate and one Traditionalist candidate.

\*\*\*

The first classroom to vote was Mr. Iola's. The voting was scheduled to take place at the end of the first week of the winter session. Each day leading up to that first vote, *The Representative* posted the same basic article, rewritten to make it sound slightly different each time.

The article was:

*In the days leading up to the first classroom's vote, polls of the two Reformist candidates show Shelly McMarton leading Percy Wethers in Mr. Iola's classroom. A win there will set the tone for Shelly and demonstrate that she is the best Reformist candidate. Talking to students in the hall and reading their comments on Facebook and on the academy discussion boards, one can see that*

*Shelly is widely viewed as the best person for the job. The students writing these things understand that experience counts for more than wishful thinking and empty promises. It would be a shame if the freshmen, who are new to the process of electing a senior class president, were to waste their vote by picking someone who won't actually be able to accomplish anything once he's elected.*

\*\*\*

In the week leading up to the first vote, Shelly McMarton, Percy Wethers, and Chet Booth all worked with their faculty advisors to get every possible vote. For McMarton, this meant remaining out of sight and letting her cavalry continue to hang posters around the academy and badmouth Percy online. For Wethers, it meant reminding everyone of the things Shelly McMarton had once supported and pointing out that her recent comments in favor of flip-flops and free laptops had only come about in the last week. For Chet Booth, it meant wearing a different type of hat to each class. Sometimes a cowboy hat, sometimes a baseball cap. He also insisted that his sister loved him.

\*\*\*

Reginald Cript was the only kid who didn't meet with his faculty advisor in that final week because he still didn't have one. He didn't even know the option existed. He also didn't realize when exactly the first class voted. Instead of trying to get everyone in Mr. Iola's class to check the box next to his name, Cript walked down the hallways making jokes about Chet's complexion, the latest movie he had seen, and about how fast he had driven to the academy in his Maserati that day.

# 2

"Okay, class. Everyone ready?"

Mr. Iola passed out a sheet of paper to each student. There was no place for them to write their name and no need for them to do so. There were only candidates' names with a checkbox next to each.

"Don't take this responsibility lightly," Mr. Iola said. "You're helping chart the course this academy will take by choosing your next senior class president."

The kids looked at the names, marked an X next to one, then folded the paper and put it in a box so the votes could be tallied.

\*\*\*

Mr. McHendricks, one of the vice principals at United Exceptionalism, read the results over the academy's public address system before the final bell sounded. None of the students needed to be told who was speaking because Mr. McHendricks sounded like he was chronically on the verge of losing his voice, croaking out every word and sipping water between each sentence.

"The first class of students has voted. For the Traditionalists, Chet Booth received thirteen votes and Reginald Cript received eleven votes." He coughed and took another bit of water. "For the Reformists, Shelly McMarton won twelve votes and Percy Wethers"—he paused, as if doubting what he was reading—"also received twelve votes. It was a tie."

\*\*\*

Later that day, Shelly posted on her Facebook page that she was thankful to the students who had voted

for her and said she looked forward to being the next
senior class president.

Percy told a gymnasium full of students, "They
never gave us a shot. Before this school year, no one even
knew who I was, and now we've tied with the person
everyone keeps trying to say is the inevitable winner." He
gave a big smile. "Well, maybe they shouldn't count us out
too soon."

Chet Booth actually cried with happiness. Not
only that, he was so elated to have gotten more votes than
Reginald that he refused to blow his nose because he
wanted each student to see how happy they had made him.

Cript told everyone that he was glad he didn't win
Mr. Iola's classroom. "They have a long history of picking
losers, so I'm really glad they picked Chet."

***

The next day, *The Representative* published this
piece:

> *United Exceptionalism held the first vote yesterday for who
> will be the Reformist and Traditionalist candidates for senior class
> president. A lot has been said about the unique nature of this year's
> race, with the most qualified candidate we may ever have running
> against a kid with grand ideas of being Santa Claus. And on the
> other side of the race, a boy no one likes is running against a rich kid
> who talks about girls in jeans (and out of them) more than he likes
> talking about the issues impacting United Exceptionalism. So it was
> no shock that the results yesterday were also unique.*
>
> *On the Traditionalist side, Chet Booth managed to pull
> out a narrow victory due to the promises he reportedly made to various
> students in Mr. Iola's classroom. Reginald Cript, unruffled by the
> loss, vowed to win every other class's votes, saying, "Chet's a loser, a
> natural born loser. It's a matter of time until the other students figure
> that out. And he's a creepy kid. Have you ever noticed how creepy he
> is?"*

*On the Reformist side, Shelly McMarton and Percy Wethers tied, which is actually a victory for Shelly. Her perseverance in wanting to make United Exceptionalism a better academy is the standard by which we should hold all of our role models to. Almost every faculty member predicts she will be the next senior class president...*

***

Yeri read the piece to himself on the floor of Anna's room while she sat on her bed and did her Calculus homework.

"Did you know that by tying Percy, Shelly actually won?"

He said this as though the mere idea was fatiguing and he needed to yawn.

Anna's face appeared from the side of her textbook. "That's not what they said, is it?"

But she could tell from his frown that it was.

She added, "You and I could write better stories than that."

3

The next class wasn't scheduled to vote until three days later. Not a single student or faculty member could explain the reasoning for this other than "it's how things have always been done." The second classroom to vote belonged to Ms. Hampen-Shiar, who taught English. Her classroom was next to Percy Wethers's homeroom so everyone thought he might do well there. Leading up to the vote, *The Representative* posted an article saying that unless Percy won by huge numbers, it should be considered a loss for him.

That day, at the end of school, Mr. McHendricks got back on the academy public address system and announced that Percy did indeed get the majority of the votes. Thirteen students voted for him and seven voted for Shelly. For the Traditionalists, only three students voted for Chet Booth. Everyone else voted for Cript.

\*\*\*

On the way home from school that day, Yeri sat in the passenger seat of Anna's Acura as she drove him home. He barely replied each time Anna said something, which wasn't like him. They were only a couple miles away from United Exceptionalism when Anna finally asked what was wrong.

"The vote today," he said. "It's bullshit."

"Percy won thirteen to seven," she said. "That's great."

He shook his head. "That's how the students voted. The teacher's vote counts for more than the students. When you include her vote, it was another tie."

Her voice dropped. "No way."

Yeri's face was the textbook image of the incorruptible spirit of youth as it was being smacked across the face.

"Way."

They rode in silence for a while before Anna said, "But that's bullshit."

"Exactly."

\*\*\*

*The Representative's* next article was posted later that evening.

*With two classrooms having voted so far for Reformist*

110

*candidates, the race is quickly turning from the question of "Will Shelly win?" to the question, "How much longer until Shelly officially wins?" Even though the students who have voted have been nearly split between McMarton and Wethers, the teachers have spoken out and nearly all of them have said they'll be supporting Shelly. Because of this, Wethers can't be happy with merely tying with McMarton any more or even winning the smaller classrooms. He'll have to start winning the remaining classrooms by large margins if he wants to have any hope of winning.*

***

If Booth took the lopsided loss hard, he didn't show it.

"Only three kids voted for you, you piece of shit," one kid yelled, a senior who had put down a hefty deposit for a tux and limo for the school dance that Chet had nearly gotten cancelled.

Chet didn't seem concerned, though.

"I'm one and one. I'm batting five hundred."

"You barely won the first classroom and you got your ass handed to you yesterday," the senior said, adding, "you dipshit," before walking away.

***

Reginald Cript didn't share the opinion that just because he had won one classroom and lost the other that he was tied with Booth.

"Chet's done," he told a group of kids at the cafeteria the next day. "He's too dumb and ugly to know he's done, but he is. I'd be surprised if he wins another classroom. Someone really needs to tell that weirdo that he should drop out. They ought to take him behind a barn and put him out of his misery."

All of the students around him roared with laughter. When it died down, someone asked Cript what he would do to help the academy if he were to become senior class president. Cript didn't have to think about the answer.

"I know more about running academies than anyone. I'd make United Exceptionalism the best damn school ever. Ever."

A senior named Debbie laughed, unsure if he was being serious or not. "You know how to run schools?"

"I know how to run everything. I've watched shows on improvements to schools. I'd flip this academy upside down so fast it'd make your head spin."

# 4

The next class to vote was Ms. Neveda's. She taught American History and had been at United Exceptionalism longer than most of the other faculty members. After handing out and the ballots, she scanned over the children sitting at each desk. After a moment, she saw two of her students whisper something to each other and then walked to Danny Auster's desk and took the form back from him.

"I'm sorry, Danny. This is supposed to be a confidential process. I saw you and Tim talking."

Usually, Danny would have scoffed at such an absurd comment. All he had said to his friend was that his pencil had broken and he needed a new one.

It took him a moment to offer any response and when he did it wasn't particularly clever: "Huh?"

Ms. Neveda reached down and took the paper off the desk and crumpled it up. She then turned and reached for the paper on Tim's desk as well. Tim's hand landed on the sheet before she could take it.

"What are you doing?" he asked.

Tim and Danny had gone to more of Percy's daily gymnasium talks than just about anyone else and were both excited to have someone as senior class president who actually seemed like a decent kid.

"Let the paper go, Tim."

His hand didn't move. "Why?"

"You broke the rules."

"He needed another pencil."

"I'm sorry, we can't make excuses."

Tim refused to let the piece of paper go. Ms. Neveda's hand grasped its edge.

"This is bullshit," Tim said.

"Okay, that's it. Go to the principal's office."

Tim stared at his teacher, then glanced over at his friend for some kind of help. Nothing could be done, though.

"This is bullshit," he said again, standing from his desk and letting his teacher take the paper.

After picking up his book bag, he kicked the edge of his chair. The hollow metal leg clanged but the desk barely moved. He paused to say something else but Ms. Neveda was already tossing the ball of paper in the trashcan.

"See you tomorrow, Tim," Ms. Neveda said.

The worst part for both Danny and Tim was that she had a genuine smile as she said it, as if this was just a minor misunderstanding and all would be forgotten when they next saw each other.

\*\*\*

The announcement over the public address system that day seemed especially difficult for Mr. McHendricks to get out through his scratchy throat.

"Ms. Neveda's class voted today for senior class president. The results were sixteen votes for Cript and six for Booth. And twelve votes for McMarton and ten for Wethers."

\*\*\*

Melissa and Rachel, Shelly's social media operatives, went to work as soon as they got back to Rachel's house and turned on her computer. They would have started while they were still at school but didn't want to waste their smart phone's precious battery power on McMarton. Melissa found the piece of paper they had used to write down all of the fake user names and passwords for the academy's discussion board.

Rachel started by signing in under the name of *True Belieber*.

*Did you guys hear about the kids in Ms. Neveda's class that freaked out and started causing problems during the vote today? Typical of Percy's Pervs.*

Melissa went next. On Facebook, she signed into an account they had created under the name *Taylor Miffed*.

*Percy's Pervs strike again. Almost got into a fight with their teacher today. Sore losers!*

For Rachel's next turn, she posted to *The Representative's* comment section under the name of a girl who had graduated the year before and whom Rachel had never liked.

*A couple of Percy's Pervs threw chairs in Ms. Neveda's class today during the vote. I heard Ms. Neveda had to run out of her classroom because she was so terrified.*

\*\*\*

*Editorial:*
*Today's voting for senior class president didn't offer any surprising results—Shelly McMarton won as everyone predicted. What was shocking, however, were the reports in Ms. Neveda's class of violence that broke out from unruly students who supported Percy*

*and were unhappy with how the voting was going. There were reports of chairs being thrown and teachers running for their safety...*

\*\*\*

After the third classroom's vote, Chet stopped going around to every table in the cafeteria and talking to other students. He didn't change tactics because his fellow students detested him; he changed because they wouldn't vote for him. Shelly was proof that it was possible to dislike someone but still vote for them. Chet didn't have that magic touch.

He would have gladly smiled at comments like "You're an asshole, go away," and "I could honestly see you shutting down the entire academy if you don't get your way, you piece of shit," if it would have led to votes. It wasn't going to, however. So instead of trying to convince any of his peers to vote for him, he instead focused on getting all of the teachers' support.

"We both know I've rubbed some people the wrong way," he would start. "But we both know that's only because I have strong convictions and I stick to those convictions. Now, Cript on the other hand, who knows what he'll say on any given day. He doesn't care about anything except being popular."

"Well, one thing's for sure," old man Phillips said, one of the English teachers. "No one can accuse you of being concerned with that."

Rather than take offense at the comment, Chet smiled and thanked the teacher for his astute observation.

"So, can I count on your vote?"

"If my choices on the Traditionalist side are you or that Reginald kid, then yes, you have my vote."

\*\*\*

Cript was many things—brash, sexist, immature,

egotistical, and oblivious to the issues impacting United Exceptionalism—but he was also a natural showman. When most kids just wanted to eat their lunch and talk about who they had a crush on, which boys might get into a fight after school, or what they were planning to do that weekend, Cript had the ability to make them forget about all of that.

"I'll tell you one thing," he said to a table full of seniors who were eating up his every word. "Shelly is so chubby and stupid, not even a lesbo version of Helen Keller would want to date her. You know who you would want to date, though?" He pulled his phone out of his pocket, handed it to the first boy, and allowed him to pass it down the line from one kid to the next. "That's an Eastern European model I hooked up with this summer. Not too bad, huh? Not the hottest girl I've hooked up with by far, but better than the girls around this school, that's for sure."

When his phone had been passed all the way around the table, he told all the boys he was going to kick Shelly McMarton's ass once he was done kicking Chet's, and then he moved on to the next table.

That table was full of junior girls who had just overheard everything Cript had said. Because of that, none of them smiled when he offered his biggest grin and said, "Hello, ladies."

He motioned for the girl at the end of the table to scoot over so he could sit down. She ignored him, though, and kept eating her bagel sandwich.

"Oh, don't pay any attention to that stuff," he said, nodding his head back at the previous table. "Just guy talk. The truth is no one likes girls more than me, and there's no one running for senior class president that the girls like more than Reginald Cript."

# 5

Ten classrooms were scheduled to vote the following week, one each morning and one each afternoon. Before Mrs. Sooth-Carol handed papers out to the students in her Civics class, she asked for a show of hands.

"Who in this class identified as a Traditionalist?"

A third of the students raised their hands. Mrs. Sooth-Carol made a note on her pad of paper.

"And who identifies as Reformist?"

Again, a third of the class raised their hands. The teacher made another series of notations.

"And who doesn't think of themselves as being part of either group?"

The final third of the students in her class raised their hands. Mrs. Sooth-Carol nodded and picked the stack of papers off her desk, then began walking around the classroom. She gave the girl at the first desk and the boy sitting behind her sheets of paper but then skipped Trevor Sittington in the third seat.

"Hey, I need one too."

"Sorry, Trevor. Only Traditionalists can vote for Traditionalists and Reformists for Reformists."

Trevor had raised his hand when the teacher asked for the students who were neither Traditional nor Reformist. His face scrunched into a ball of confusion.

"Who do I get to vote for?"

The teacher shrugged. "No one. Sorry."

She handed pieces of paper out to two thirds of the class, skipping each boy and girl who said they didn't consider themselves to be a part of either main group.

Terry Boller, a boy in the middle of the classroom, raised his hand.

"Yes, Terry?"

"This isn't how the other classes did their voting."

Mrs. Sooth-Carol offered a polite smile. "It's how we're doing it in this classroom."

\*\*\*

The same thing happened in another class that voted at the end of the day. A third of the students were left without anyone to vote for.

An hour later, a different vice principal, Ms. Chorendowski, began to speak across the public address system.

"The results are in from today's two classes. In Mrs. Sooth-Carol's class, Shelly McMarton received nine votes and Percy Wethers received three votes. Reginald Cript received eight votes and Chet Booth received four votes. In Mr. Aiyama's class, McMarton received eleven votes and Wethers received two votes. Cript received ten votes and Booth received three votes."

\*\*\*

*We at The Representative have covered every race for senior class president, and yet we may never have seen a candidate who is promising so much he can't possibly deliver. Here are ten reasons why Percy Wethers's ideas are nothing but wishful thinking...*

\*\*\*

Anna read the latest piece posted on *The Representative*'s website and shook her head.

"Why don't they just come out and say, 'For the next couple weeks all we're going to do is push our opinions on you instead of delivering actual news'? That would be more honest than what they're doing."

Yeri shook his head. "They should change the name of the paper to the *McMarton Times*."

\*\*\*

The first classroom to vote the following day was one of the many that Shelly McMarton claimed to be her homeroom. She easily won. That was followed in the afternoon by Ms. Louisa's class. Without asking what group each student identified with, Ms. Louisa began handing out sheets of paper only to certain students.

Matt Kruger raised his hand.

"Yes, Matt?"

"Uh, I'd like a ballot too."

"Sorry, if you remember, each student filled out a form at the beginning of the school year. On that form you said you didn't want to be considered as a Traditionalist or a Reformist. That means you can't vote in this round."

"But I'm a Reformist now."

"Sorry, it's too late to change."

\*\*\*

Vice Principal Chorendowski came back on the academy's public address system at the end of the day.

"In Mr. Ark's class, Shelly McMarton won ten votes and Percy Wethers won five. Reginald Cript won eight and Chet Booth won seven. In Ms. Louisa's class, McMarton received nine votes and Wethers received four. Reginald Cript received eight votes and Booth received five votes."

\*\*\*

"Why is Chet Booth still in the race?" Cript yelled down the hallway as school was letting out. "He has no shame. Zero. If I was getting my ass kicked as bad as that kid, you wouldn't see my face here ever again. That won't happen, though, because I don't lose. I bet you can look at Chet's baby photos and see his parents making L's with their hands and putting them in front of their foreheads as they laughed at poor Anus-Face Chet."

# 6

A pattern had begun to form. In the classes with mostly juniors or seniors, Shelly had a clear advantage. In the classes with mostly freshmen or sophomores, Percy was favored. When teachers allowed anyone in their class to vote, Percy usually won. When the teacher restricted voting to only students who had said they were Reformist, Shelly would win.

The pattern wasn't as clear on the Traditionalist side. Booth tended to do better in the classrooms with students whose parents had also attended United Exceptionalism. Even when he did win it was by a narrow margin. Cript won all of the other classrooms, with two or three times more votes than Chet.

\*\*\*

Only a quarter of the classrooms at United Exceptionalism had voted for their choice of senior class president when *The Representative* posted a slew of stories, at least one each day, that all had the same general message.

*A large section of the academy has spoken. What have they said? That they're ready for Shelly McMarton to become their next senior class president. Yes, only a portion of United Exceptionalism has voted. And yes, Percy Wethers has done better than anyone thought he would. But Shelly has received more votes, and when you factor in the weighted votes of the faculty, the race isn't close. The race is, by all standards, effectively over.*

\*\*\*

"I guess we don't need to vote," Anna said, regretting having wasted time reading *The Representative's* latest post.

Yeri leaned over and gave her a kiss for no better reason than he wanted to. He also knew from Anna's tone that she was being sarcastic and he loved this side of her.

"Why's that?"

Anna tossed her phone back in her backpack and said, "Didn't you hear? The race is supposedly already over."

\*\*\*

Percy was the first to admit he had gotten trounced in some of the classrooms, especially a couple of the classes near Shelly's homeroom. But he had also won many of the contests and believed he could win more.

"If we stick together," he told kids gathered on the gym's bleachers, "if we don't give up, and we continue to get our message out, we can make this the type of academy everyone's proud of."

Looking out at the gym, though, he noticed that there were fewer students than had been there previously. It wasn't a sizable drop off, only a dozen or two fewer kids. He hoped no one else would notice.

"We just need to stick together," he said again. "When this school was founded, no one person did it on their own. It took a team. At each key moment in United Exceptionalism's distinguished academic history, change was only achieved when the students came together behind a common cause. Well, I'm asking you to stand with me now."

Just like they always did, the students cheered.

***

Booth was a lot of things, but he wasn't stupid. He knew he was losing to Cript and that it was only a matter of time until the election was over and he had lost. Appealing to segments of the student body by acting and dressing like them hadn't worked. Getting the backing of the faculty had worked to a limited extent, but not enough. The only thing left to do was to become more like the boy he was running against. Cript went around talking about how girls who wore jeans were sluts and a large segment of the student body ate it up. Cript also went around making fun of everyone and everything, and the kids liked that as well. Booth knew what he had to do.

The next time *The Representative* sent a reporter to talk to him about his campaign, he started off by saying, "I don't think it's fair that Cript is getting all of this attention for what he's saying about girls in jeans. I've been saying the same thing for years."

The reporter, Betsy Shonenberg-Newcastle, was the same freshman Cript had publicly humiliated. Although she claimed to be impartial, part of her hoped Chet found a way to beat Cript after the way Reginald had berated her in the hallway. The problem, however, was that Chet had never said anything of the sort before.

"Have you mentioned this to anyone else?" she asked.

"No, I mean, yes." Chet gave a creepy wink and smile, which made Betsy shiver. "I talked about it with my friends, but I didn't think it was the type of thing that was appropriate to discuss openly during the campaign. Now that I see Cript talking about it, though, I figured it was okay to let everyone know I agree."

Something about what Chet had just said made Betsy frown.

"Wait, you have friends?"

Chet nodded and his smile widened like a python's. For a moment, it looked like he might try to put Betsy's face in his mouth. His hands waved the question away.

"That's not important. What is important is that the students at United Exceptionalism understand I was the one who came up with the idea first. Girls who wear denim are whores."

Betsy flinched. When she wasn't at school, she liked to wear jeans.

"Are you getting this?" Chet asked, noticing she wasn't writing everything down.

Betsy's pencil burst into life, jotting notes until they filled her paper.

"Yeah, I got it," she said.

***

Cript was having a grand time. Everywhere he went he was even more of a celebrity than he had been before the campaign started. He knew a large portion of the students were disgusted by the things he was saying, but he also knew there were just as many kids who loved what he stood for. It was easy to ignore the ones who gave him dirty looks because there were always other students nearby who adored him.

Understanding that any attention was good attention, Cript made an effort to say at least one outrageous thing each day. On the surface, it made him look unpredictable, a loose cannon who could say anything at any time. But in reality, most everything he said was calculated to get the response he was looking for.

One day he went around making critical blanket statements about the kids from the other nearby schools. Another day he went around doing impressions of what Chet Booth would be like if he were from other countries.

This consisted mainly of speaking in a stereotypical accent and saying he liked to eat that country's traditional food.

"*Bon jour*, my name-ah is Chet Booth, and I sure-ah do love deez frog's legs to go in my goblin mouth!"

Most kids realized this was all part of Cript's shtick and so they either ignored it if they didn't like him or else they laughed if they did like him.

However, two things in particular brought much more attention on him than even he planned for. The first was his comment, seemingly serious, that Chet Booth might not be eligible to be senior class president of United Exceptionalism.

"All I'm saying is I heard he's been homeschooled part of the time. If you're homeschooled, are you allowed to be senior class president? I don't know the answer, I'm just asking the question."

For a week, Cript said he had experts investigating whether Chet Booth was actually eligible to become senior class president.

The other thing he said that made every jaw drop was that he would gladly date his own little sister if she weren't related to him.

"You're kidding, right?" one of the boys asked, laughing.

The students at all of the nearby tables stopped their conversations and began whispering about what Cript had just said.

Reginald shook his head. "Absolutely not. She's super cute. Really hot. I'd date her in two seconds if she wasn't my little sister."

Another boy said, "Dude, she's only in eighth grade. She's not even in high school yet."

Cript shook his head in confusion. "Hot is hot. It doesn't matter how old she is."

Even Reginald's biggest supporters weren't sure why he felt the need to say that.

7

The second-largest classroom to vote was one in which Percy knew a lot of the students. Prior to the vote, the teacher, Mr. Yoark, told a quarter of the class that he had lost the papers they had filled out at the beginning of the year stating which group they included themselves in.

Robert Hannigan raised his hand. "That's no problem. We can all tell you right now. I'm a Reformist."

Before any other student joined in and the class got sidetracked, Mr. Yoark motioned for silence. "It's not that easy. We can't re-do the paperwork now. I'm afraid you won't get to vote this year."

It seemed so easy to get a blank piece of paper and fill out which group each student aligned with that the entire class waited for their teacher to say he was joking.

Growing impatient, Meg Chatwood raised her hand. "Why do we even need to say which group we're in? Why can't we just vote?"

The rest of the class was still so convinced that Mr. Yoark was pranking them that they sat quietly, waiting for their chance to vote for senior class president.

"I'm sorry," Mr. Yoark said. "We have rules that we have to abide by. I admit it's my fault that the papers were lost and I wish there was something I could do, but it's too late. You can vote again next year, though."

\*\*\*

Vice Principal McHendricks coughed out each word as he gave the day's election results over the public address system.

"In Mr. Yoark's class today, Shelly McMarton received eighteen votes and Percy Wethers received fourteen. For the Traditionalists, Reginald Cript received twenty-eight votes and Chet Booth received four."

\*\*\*

Anna asked if Yeri had heard about what happened in Mr. Yoark's class.

"Yeah, but only because Charlie told me. If you read *The Representative*, you'd never know how many kids weren't allowed to vote because of some mix-up."

"Marie told me they've had a bunch of things like that happen in other classes too."

"Unless you're in those classes or are friends with someone who is, you'd never know."

Anna squeezed Yeri's hand.

"So let's do something about it."

Yeri kissed her cheek and asked what she had in mind.

"Let's start our own paper." Her eyes flashed with excitement. "How many times have we read *The Representative* and thought we could do a better job?" When she saw his eyebrows arch in confusion, she added, "Not a real paper, of course. Nothing in print. But we could start our own Facebook page and put in stories about what's actually going on at the academy. We could even ask Ms. Yealdon if we can get class credit for doing it."

"God, you're so incredible," Yeri said, kissing her.

He asked where they should start and her response was immediate. "Find out which students weren't allowed to vote today, ask who they would have voted for, and then see if that would have impacted the results."

\*\*\*

Each time a kid asked Shelly McMarton how she thought the election was going, she gave the same response: "United Exceptionalism can't afford a senior class president like Cript. We really need to rally together and make sure he isn't elected."

This garnered one of two reactions. From the students who were talking to her out of sheer politeness, they merely shrugged and said, "Oh, cool," and walked off. From everyone else, the response was, "But what about your race against Percy Wethers?"

To this, Shelly inevitably laughed.

"Oh, that race? That was done before it started."

\*\*\*

*As the election continues, and as Percy Wethers's chances of victory become more unrealistic, we at The Representative have to wonder how much longer he's going to stay in the race. He's done a lot of good for the Reformists by making Shelly become a better candidate for senior class president. But now that he's facing an insurmountable mountain to climb, it seems like the only decent thing to do would be for him to drop out so Shelly can begin to focus on defeating Cript and becoming the next senior class president at United Exceptionalism.*

\*\*\*

The longer the first round of voting went on, the more Chet Booth crumbled under the pressure. He told an entire class of students that they were "fairies." (One of the students in that class *still* voted for him.) He told another classroom that he was glad he didn't have to share a homeroom with them because they were all of questionable character. (No one in that class voted for him.)

The lowest point might have been when a video of him picking his nose and then putting the finger in his mouth was posted on Facebook.

\*\*\*

Cript didn't hold back just because he was winning. The more attention he got, the more he craved being the constant topic of conversation at every lunch table.

Angie Champion was the next reporter sent by *The Representative* to talk with Reginald about his views. After the way he had treated Betsy, culminating in her being blacklisted, Angie was determined to ask him the questions she had prepared and get out of there as fast as possible.

"Chet Booth recently said he was the first person to talk about banning jeans. How do you feel about that?"

Although Reginald might start yelling, Angie knew this was the type of question Cript loved because it would give him a chance to go on a tirade that would ultimately lead him to talking endlessly about himself.

"Let me tell you something, Angie. Goblin Face Chet has gotten to the point where he has to say the same things as me in hopes of getting attention. It's sad, and it's not working. If anyone is talking about him, it's about him eating his own boogers."

Even though she hadn't wanted to, she couldn't help but smile. After all, the image of the snot between Chet's teeth *had* been funny. Disgusting, but funny. After receiving the reaction he'd been looking for, Cript continued.

"You're a lot better than that Bitchy Betsy, that's for sure. I was beginning to think the only girls that *The Representative* was going to send over would be on the rag. Don't get me wrong, I can handle it. I'm a fighter."

Angie stared at her notes, unsure what to say next. Betsy was one of her best friends, but at the moment she didn't want to mention that fact. She only wanted to get out of the interview.

"Uh, so you're really serious about girls who wear jeans?"

"That they're sluts? Absolutely. Listen, we have to

get them out of here. Whether that's changing the dress code or putting them in a corner and buildings screens around them, I don't know."

"Who would pay for the screens?"

She knew she sounded stupid, but she couldn't fathom what the answer would be.

"We'll make the girls' parents pay for them."

# 8

"I don't know about you," Shelly McMarton said to a table of senior girls who looked past her with disinterest, "but I'm sickened, absolutely sickened, by what Cript has been saying about some of the girls in this academy."

"What about Percy Wethers?" one of the girls asked in between bites of an apple.

Shelly cocked her head to one side. "What about him?"

"Aren't you running against him right now?"

Another girl said, "Didn't he win two of the last four classroom elections?"

Shelly smiled, genuinely amused by the naïve questions. "Oh, that. Yeah, I'm grateful to him for increasing awareness on many of the issues I've been talking about for years. But what we really need to focus on is making sure Reginald Cript isn't elected as senior class president."

*\*\*\**

*In its long and distinguished history as the finest academic institution in this wonderful country, we at The Representative have seen many students who aspired to become senior class president. Each of them was unique in some way or another but none of them has ever proposed something as shocking as what Reginald Cript has suggested this year when he said all girls who wear jeans are promiscuous (to put it nicely) and should either be kicked out of school or placed in the corner of each classroom with a screen put up around them. That kind of rhetoric not only goes against the ideas that United Exceptionalism was founded on, it's dangerous and divides us. The most troubling aspect is that this kind of outrageousness is the norm for Cript.*

\*\*\*

Even with *The Representative* insisting that Shelly had already won and that it was a matter of time until Percy dropped out, students still attended his gymnasium talks and cheered as he decried the way United Exceptionalism was being run to benefit the faculty and alumni rather than how it should be run—to benefit the students. In a shocking twist, a member of the faculty, Mrs. A'wai, one of the Physical Education teachers, decided to support Percy. Mrs. A'wai's homeroom had less influence than any other class and she was only one of the fifty full-time teachers, but her support was a sign that Percy wasn't going away.

Later in the day, a poll in *The Representative* showed how the general student population felt about each candidate. Students were asked to ignore whether or not they agreed with a candidate's ideas and vote purely on whether or not they had a favorable opinion of that person. Chet Booth came in last place, with only twenty-seven percent of the students having a favorable opinion of him. Reginald Cript was next, with thirty-one percent of students liking him. Shelly McMarton was next with thirty-three percent of students liking her. Percy Wethers finished first, with almost seventy percent of students saying they had a favorable opinion of him.

# The Faulty Process of Electing a Senior Class President

\*\*\*

*The Representative* gave an interesting spin on the results.

*There are some key points from today's favorability poll that need to be discussed. The first is that a good senior class president shouldn't care about being liked or not; it's simply not part of the job. The most important part of leading the academy is doing what's best for the school, and the person with the experience to do that is clearly Shelly McMarton. She's the candidate for senior class president who provides a consistent and realistic message. When you attend one of Percy's rallies in the gymnasium, you get the sense that he's more concerned with being liked than with actually helping United Exceptionalism. Shelly, to her credit, has never been concerned with what the students think about her; she's too focused on actually getting things done to worry about popularity. That's the sign of a true leader and someone who would make a great senior class president.*

\*\*\*

The next day, Yeri and Anna went to Ms. Yealdon's classroom before any other students had arrived. All around the walls were pictures of the legends of journalism from both print and television. Each of them was smiling in their photograph even though all they did was cover the dregs of society, the failings of the human race, and the politicians who never did anything about any of it.

Neither Yeri nor Anna was one of Ms. Yealdon's students, so they had to start by introducing themselves. Looking puzzled, the Journalism teacher asked what she could do.

"We'd like to start a newspaper and write for it. We were hoping we could get school credit for our time."

Ms. Yealdon frowned. "We have a paper, *The Representative*. You could write for that if the editor needs extra help, but you wouldn't receive school credit unless you signed up for Journalism in the spring semester."

"We know about the school paper," Anna said, a little too eagerly. "We were hoping to start a different paper."

Up to that point, Ms. Yealdon had been focusing most of her attention on a mug of coffee that was billowing steam toward her nose. Hearing this, she put the mug down and looked directly at both students.

"Why on earth would you start another paper when we already have one?"

Yeri offered a smile before saying, "Have you ever noticed everything they write has the same message? All of the attention is given to Reginald Cript and none to any other Traditionalists. No matter what happens, Shelly McMarton is great and Percy Wethers is awful. And most of the time whatever the alumni and faculty want is made to sound great and whatever the students want is ignored or discounted? We wanted to start a paper that gives the opposite view."

Ms. Yealdon blew on her coffee. After taking another sip, she let out a long sigh.

"Well, I can't tell you what to do or what not to do; I can only say I wouldn't be able to offer class credit for a hobby like that. And I'd caution you to think about all the things you may have overlooked, such as why students would read it, how they would find out about it in the first place, all the time and effort it takes to put a paper together, and the editing process that ensures a good product. When you factor all of that in, it quickly becomes overwhelming." She took another sip of her coffee and then smiled. "But if that's how you want to spend your time, more power to you."

\*\*\*

On the other end of the campus, Chet Booth was meeting with his faculty advisor, who was none too happy with him.

Mr. Stove said, "I don't know what you were thinking. I'd hazard a guess that you weren't thinking at all."

Chet could have explained again that by mimicking Cript's speaking points he was trying to steal the other boy's followers away from him. He could have said that any publicity was good publicity. But he had already said both things and Mr. Stove wasn't buying it.

"I'm going to let you in on a secret, Chet. You have no charisma. Zero. That's why Reginald can say something outrageous and get away with it and you can't. If you had even an ounce of self-awareness you'd realize that."

"So what do I do?"

Mr. Stove shook his head and dug the knuckles of his index fingers into the corners of his eyes.

"At this point, I'd be quiet and hope Cript does or says something that gets himself expelled from school. Outside of that, I'd plan on transferring to another academy. You'd have a better chance of getting elected some place where no one knows you."

\*\*\*

"You'd really put all the girls in jeans in a corner and put screens around them?"

It was the hundredth time a student had asked the question of Cript. A couple of times it was from a girl who was wearing denim and couldn't hide her disdain. But much more often it was from kids who either thought the idea was hilarious, regardless of how little sense it made, or students who for one reason or another had a personal bias against some of the girls at school. This time it was asked by a senior boy who laughed at the idea of his little sister being sequestered in the back corner of class. Several other seniors at the table looked on in amusement.

"You're damn right I would," Cript said with a grin. "I'd put every single one of those jean-wearing floozies in a corner where they belong and build a wall right around their fat asses. This is United Exceptionalism. If they want to do away with the dress code that made this academy great, we'll do away with their ugly faces."

Even though all of the boys were friends with girls who wore jeans to school or had little sisters who did, they all slapped their knees and chuckled. None of them actually thought the plan would be enacted. They just liked to imagine the absurdity of it.

"You really think you can tell their parents they have to pay for their own daughters to be placed behind screens?"

It was the type of question that could elicit two drastically different answers from Reginald. If asked by a female reporter from *The Representative*, he might berate her and tell her to go overdose on personality pills so someone had a chance of actually liking her. But at a table full of boys who clearly enjoyed everything he had to say, he laughed and nodded.

"Of course. They won't have a choice. They can send their daughters to another academy but it won't be a school as good as United Exceptionalism. Or they can dress their daughters in the types of clothes the academy's founders would have approved of. Or they can sit in a corner and not be seen. When you think about it that way, I'm being perfectly reasonable."

The boys laughed again. However, none of them could pinpoint what was so funny about the last thing Reginald had said. They didn't realize that what was making them laugh wasn't what Cript said but the way he said it. He was talking about taking a segment of the student body and humiliating them by putting them in the corner of the classroom and placing a barrier around them. And yet he sounded like he honestly believed it was reasonable. That was what was so incredibly funny to the teenagers—not that Cript was being a bully and a monster but that he could make those things seem feasible.

"And you know what else we'll have to do?" Cript asked. The boys all waited for the next line. "We'll have to build a special wall for Chet Booth's ugly goblin face. That thing is ugly. I mean u-g-l-y. And we'll make his parents pay for that, too."

# 9

Either Ms. Yealdon was trying to intimidate Yeri and Anna or she didn't realize how much times had changed. It was actually very easy for the young couple to start their own paper. It was really just a blog, but they liked thinking of it as an underground school paper. Yeri tweeted the blog's website to his friends and Anna tweeted it to her friends. After those kids retweeted it, it had already reached nearly a quarter of the school.

Coming up with a name for their site had been the hardest part. After suggestions like *Academy Diaries*, *The Academy Papers*, and *Exceptional Updates*, Anna suggested the name they finally went with. *Notes from the Underground.*

The first entry covered the favorability polls that the editor of *The Representative* had discussed, but took the opposite stance.

*Recently, our academy's newspaper provided statistics on how the student body views each of the four main candidates running for senior class president. Their conclusion was that it's the mark of a good senior class president to not worry about being liked. Is that really how far we've gone from the days of institutions having people they could be proud of? Shelly McMarton does have the experience necessary to become senior class president, but why would United Exceptionalism want someone to serve as the most important role if only one third of students can say anything nice about her? The same goes for Chet Booth and Reginald Cript, both of whom have similarly unenthusiastic favorability numbers. The shocking thing to see this year isn't how the faculty and alumni work so hard to convince students that one candidate is better than another, it's that they work so hard to convince us that the only candidate with excellent favorability numbers is wrong for the future of our academy...*

***

Anna and Yeri followed up their first post by searching for Shelly when they got to school the next day. They found her by her locker.

"Hi, Shelly," Anna said. "My boyfriend and I are starting a new school paper and we wanted to see if you'd like to be interviewed."

"No, thanks," Shelly said, not looking away from the stack of books in her locker. "You can talk to my faculty advisor if you want. He can answer questions for you."

McMarton took two textbooks out and put them in her bag, then removed two from her backpack and put those in the locker.

"It would be a great way for the students to see a different side of you," Yeri said.

"I said, no thanks."

With that, Shelly closed her locker and walked off to her next class.

Anna gave an exasperated sigh. "And she wonders why no one likes her."

***

After the last class of the day, the couple found Wethers and asked the same of him. After being dismissed by Shelly, both Yeri and Anna had their eyebrows raised, unsure of what response to expect. Percy turned from the group of kids he was talking to and looked at them.

"You've both been to some of my gymnasium talks." A smile stretched across Percy's face. "I'd love to talk to you."

He walked with them to the library, which was unoccupied except for the librarian, who was putting books away. Percy told them about what first made him become interested in running for senior class president. He reviewed all the poor decisions in United Exceptionalism's recent history that Shelly had supported and that he had been against and he mentioned all the ways he could improve the academy. No matter what they asked, he waved his hands around and gave excited answers.

Sometimes, after a question, he would say, "An even better question is," and then answer that or he would say "The real problem is," and then go on about what he could do to make United Exceptionalism better. The few times he didn't fully answer their questions the first time, he apologized and answered again.

They went like that for what seemed to be less than an hour, but when Yeri checked his watch, two hours had gone by. The library was deserted and quiet. Even the librarian had left for the day.

"I could talk about this stuff all night," Percy said.

***

The article that Yeri and Anna posted to *Notes from the Underground* was only online for a couple minutes when it started to receive attention. Unfortunately for them, it wasn't the type of response they were hoping for.

Dozens of comments were posted, one after another, and only three of them were positive. The other thirty or forty all said that whoever wrote the blog was obviously a Percy's Perv and that there was no point in reading something by someone who was clearly playing favorites. Anyone who wanted fair and unbiased reporting should read *The Representative*, they said. Some pointed out the one typo that existed in the blog entry. Others made fun of Yeri and Anna for spending their time posting about Percy Wethers instead of having actual lives like other teenagers. Still others said how Percy was way behind in the academy's voting and should just drop out.

Neither Yeri nor Anna had any way of knowing that all of the negative comments were posted by only two people. The saddest part was that Anna considered Melissa and Rachel, the two girls posting everything, to be her friends.

\*\*\*

Chet Booth didn't know Anna or Yeri except from the photos the couple had posted to *Notes from the Underground*. Because of this, he had to ask around to find out where he could find the new reporters. No one he asked wanted to speak to him.

When he did finally find them outside their Chemistry class, he asked if he could be interviewed for their blog and they agreed. Just like they had done with Percy, they decided to meet in the library.

"Thanks for agreeing to interview me," Chet said with a pleasant smile, and Anna found herself thinking that maybe everything she had heard about Chet was wrong.

Anna asked the first question. "What made you decide you wanted to run for senior class president?"

"Well, let me tell you, let me just say how much of a disaster our current senior class president is. We can't afford another year of somebody like that and that's exactly what Shelly McMarton is. She'd be a disaster. An epic disaster of apocalyptic proportions!"

Yeri and Anna both took deep breaths.

"Okay," Yeri said. "So you think Shelly will be bad for United Exceptionalism. But what is it about you that makes you the good choice other than not being her."

"We need someone," Chet said, his head bobbing with energy, "who will return this academy to the ideas it was founded on. The men who founded this school knew what it took to make great high school graduates. The academy has gotten away from that and will keep getting further away if we choose someone like Shelly or Cript."

"I understand, but what will you do?"

This seemed to confuse Chet slightly. It took him a moment to find an answer.

"Well, I'll get the academy back to the core values it was founded on."

Anna checked her notes before saying, "The founders, many of them anyway, were slave owners who used slave labor to construct the buildings we use..."

Chet's face lost all of its color. "Nothing like that! I mean the other values."

"Such as?"

Chet's gaze darted all around the library until he finally settled on an appropriate response. "What we really need to talk about is how much of a disaster Reginald Cript would be as the Traditionalist candidate."

***

Cript accepted Anna and Yeri's invitation for an interview but as he always did he refused to answer questions unless they came to his father's mansion to ask them.

"Holy shit," Anna said. "So this is how the other half lives."

"To most people in the world," Yeri said, "you and I are the other half as well. Cript is in a category of his own."

To their side, a family of deer watched them from the edge of the woods and then sauntered back into the brush. In front of them, a giant fountain let water cascade over three tiers of pools. To their other side, a five-car garage kept the Cript family's expensive automobiles out of sight.

They rang the doorbell and waited. They were on time and both of them could hear someone on the other side of the door. Anna wondered if Cript was making them wait just because he could. They rang the doorbell a second time and waited another two minutes. Finally, the heavy wooden door opened.

"Welcome to my humble abode," Cript said with a smile, offering no explanation or apology for taking so long to answer the door.

"Thanks for agreeing to the interview," Yeri said. "We'd really like the academy to have a second option for where they get their news from and—"

"Would you like some water or orange juice?" Cript said, not even realizing his guest had been speaking.

"I'll take some water, thanks," Anna said.

Cript pointed to the kitchen. "The glasses are in the second cabinet from the left."

"Oh."

She walked to the kitchen and filled a glass with water while Yeri opened his backpack and got out his cell phone to record anything he missed with pen and paper. When Anna came back, she sat beside Yeri on a white sofa with a gold table beside it.

"What made you want to become senior class president?" Yeri asked.

Cript leaned back against the chair he was sitting on. "The academy is going to hell in a handbag. We have a senior class president who's out of touch. He's weak. We have problems affecting United Exceptionalism that no one wants to talk about, let alone fix. I'm the man to fix them."

"Problems like girls wearing jeans?" Anna asked.

"Exactly," Cript said, his voice echoing slightly in the oversized living room. "It's a shame our academy has gotten to the point where we have girls in jeans being a distraction. We either need to get rid of them or put screens around them."

"Out of sight, out of mind?" Yeri said with a cringe.

Anna's face contorted with irritation for a moment before she realized Yeri was just trying to get Reginald to continue talking.

"See? I knew you'd understand," Cript said. "Not like those fat pigs from *The Representative*. That place has too much estrogen. They need a testosterone injection, if you know what I mean."

Anna grimaced and squirmed, but Reginald seemed not to notice. Then he went on about how he'd never seen any of the girls from *The Representative* actually go on dates, paused for effect, and then added, "With boys, at least," and winked at Yeri as if he'd understand what he was saying.

"So," Anna said, "On the topic of Jorge M. Shrub ordering the football team to beat up the kids at Iroquois Regional High School—you were against that?"

"Of course I was. That's exactly the type of bad judgment we've had for too long from our senior class presidents. They had no plan. They just sent our players in there to beat up everyone they could find. They had zero idea of what would happen after the football team was done."

She pulled out her phone and tapped the screen a couple times.

"How do you explain this video, then, of a party from two years ago in which you say that what the football team did was great?"

She held the phone out toward Reginald so he could see the video with the little YouTube insignia at the bottom corner. In the clip, which only lasted twenty seconds, a group of boys were in a luxurious kitchen drinking out of red cups. All of them were laughing and clearly drunk. In the video, a boy shouted, "Those fucking kids at Iroquois High had it coming. They're lucky it was the football team that went there and not some of the guys my dad knows." All the other boys cheered. The video ended.

Cript shrugged. "Wasn't me."

"It sure did look and sound like you."

"It wasn't, though. I've always been against what the football team did."

She tapped on the phone again and let him watch the video a second time. After a few seconds, he checked his watch and looked around for something else to keep his interest. When the video was over, she asked if he noticed anything the second time he watched it.

"That it wasn't me?" he said, offering a fake yawn.

"It was taped in your kitchen. Same cabinets. Same countertop."

Yeri looked back and forth between Reginald, who he couldn't stand but had to be nice to for the sake of the interview, and his girlfriend, who he loved more than ever.

Reginald sighed and shook his head. "I see how this is going to be. You're going to call me a liar in my own house."

"I'm not calling you a liar, I'm just asking you to explain how—"

"Well, no one calls Reginald Cript a liar, especially not in his own home." He stood and straightened his shirt. "Get the fuck out. Both of you. And don't waste any more of my time with your silly little blog, you fucking losers. You're blacklisted."

# 10

More classroom elections took place. After thirty-seven of the fifty classes had voted, Shelly had won eighteen, Percy had won sixteen, and they had tied three times. On the Traditionalist side, Reginald Cript had won twenty-four and Chet Booth had managed to win thirteen.

\*\*\*

The next article to appear on *The Representative* began:

*Roughly three quarters of the students at United Exceptionalism have voted and, at this point in the process, Shelly McMarton's lead is insurmountable. Percy is correct in pointing out that he has won nearly as many classrooms as his opponent, but when you factor in all the votes Shelly has earned from the teachers, the race isn't close. It's time for Percy to drop out of the race. All he's doing by staying in is hurting Shelly's chances against the eventual Traditionalist candidate.*

\*\*\*

The next article to appear on *Notes from the Underground* began:

*If you read The Representative, you find Percy Wethers being called upon to drop out of the race for senior class president even though he's won almost as many classrooms as Shelly. What's curious is that the same paper isn't calling upon Chet Booth to drop out even though Reginald Cript is running away on the Traditionalist side. Why might that be? Quite simply because the faculty and alumnus know what they can expect from Shelly, and they like what they see. That's why they don't care about any of the other candidates (except for reporting on anything outrageous that Cript says because they know it will get them a lot of readers). Shelly is their pick and anyone standing in her way to becoming the next senior class president is a nuisance. Once Cript defeats Booth, they will treat him the same way.*

*The sad thing is Shelly is only winning by so much because of the unfair influence that the teachers have on the process. Even though the teachers' votes don't count until after all of the classrooms have voted and even though until then each teacher can change their mind on who they'll support, The Representative insists on adding them to the current tally in order to skew the results and make it seem like an otherwise close race is almost over. Shelly is leading— that's a fact—but by no means is her lead insurmountable, as some would have you believe.*

***

As much as they had whined about spending their time behind a computer, Melissa and Rachel both had to admit they were having immense amounts of fun posting anonymous messages to various websites. There was something completely liberating about pretending to be someone else. They could say whatever they wanted (as long as it supported Shelly somehow), and they could be anyone they wanted (as long as it was someone with a connection to United Exceptionalism).

On *The Representative's* comment section, they posted thirty-seven messages, one for each classroom that had voted so far. Some of them were:

Johnny Bragg, posted 5:56pm – *As always, great reporting from The Representative. I used to like some of what Percy Wethers said but now he just seems selfish by staying in the race.*

Jane Doe, posted 5:57pm – *The only reason, THE ONLY REASON, for Percy to stay in the race is because he's bitter or sexist or both. I bet all those Percy's Pervs are cheering him on just because they all hate girls and can't stand to see one become the next senior class president.*

Dee-Dee, posted 5:59pm – *Personally, I think it shows how great of a person Shelly is that she's allowing Percy to stay in the race even though he doesn't have a chance.*

Bruce Chub, posted 6:02pm – *Percy supporters be like, "Do I still get a free laptop if he loses?"*

The two girls then went over to the comment section of *Notes from the Underground* and started the process all over again. Some of those were:

Shelly Fan, posted 6:25pm – *It hurts my brain to read how awful the writing is here. How can you expect anyone to take this stuff seriously?*

Percy's #1 Perv, posted 6:26pm – *I like Percy, I really do, but I can't understand why he's still in the race. Just look at the latest post from The Representative. It's obvious he's already lost.*

Jean Grey, posted 6:28pm – *Wow, the "journalism" here is awful. I use that term lightly. Have you ever actually taken one of Ms. Yealdon's classes? They could help you tremendously.*

The Truth, posted 6:30pm – *Percy lost. Get over it.*

\*\*\*

Chet Booth held an open discussion after school. Everyone was invited to join him in the cafeteria to talk about the issues impacting United Exceptionalism. One sophomore walked past, saw there was no free food, and then continued down the hallway. No one else showed up.

\*\*\*

On the other side of town, Cript rented out the entire dining room of Big Pete's Crab Shack and paid for everyone to eat as many crab legs as humanly possible.

A van full of girls, some of whom didn't actually attend United Exceptionalism, pulled into the parking lot. All of them were wearing jeans. They were all also wearing t-shirts with various sayings like, "Make United Exceptionalism Denim Again" and "Build A Barrier Around Cript's Hate."

The first fight broke out before they could get into the Crab Shack. A group of girls from United Exceptionalism did the work while Cript and dozens of boys cheered them on.

"Punch her in the nose," Cript yelled to one girl as she pulled the hair of a girl wearing jeans.

The boys on either side of Cript hooted and hollered at the entire disgraceful display.

"I wish I could get out there and beat the shit out of a few of them myself," Cript said to the boy next to him.

After a couple of minutes, staff from the restaurant went outside and broke up the fight.

"Don't worry," Cript called to the girls from United Exceptionalism. Some had scratches and bruises. One had a bloody lip. Another was missing a chunk of her hair. "My dad will pay your legal bills!"

# 11

For the Traditionalists, Cript won all six of the next classrooms, leaving Booth with no shot of winning. On the Reformist side, McMarton won four of the next six. Percy was down by four classrooms and with nine to go, but one of them was the largest class in all of United Exceptionalism. Even so, the next article from *The Representative* had the following announcement:

*Shelly McMarton is the winner of the Reformists! She's won enough classrooms and enough votes from teachers to be declared the Reformist pick for senior class president.*

***

Since Yeri and Anna weren't getting credit for writing articles and thus couldn't take time out from their other classes, they had to wait until the end of the school day to post on *Notes from the Underground.*

*Don't believe what you've been hearing about the race already being over. Percy is losing, that much is true, but neither he nor Shelly will have enough votes through the classroom voting to win the election for senior class president outright. It's going to take the votes of the faculty, who don't cast their ballots until after the final classroom has had their say. And don't forget, the faculty can change their mind on who they support at anytime. Don't let a false announcement discourage you from voting.*

***

It was too little, too late. James and Aaron heard

the bell ring, yet neither rushed to make it to Mr. Fornia's class. The longtime friends were juniors at United Exceptionalism and wanted nothing more than to know their final year at the academy would be filled with good memories and fun times. Instead, it looked like Shelly McMarton and Reginald Cript were going to be their choices in the second round of voting. That was why neither bothered to get to Mr. Fornia's class to vote.

"Fuck it," James said. "It's over anyway."

Aaron didn't disagree. He was still confused, though, how Shelly could have already won if the voting had been close and a good portion of classrooms still hadn't voted.

"Yeah, waste of time."

Instead of filling out a ballot, they sat out in the hallway and played on their phones.

***

Terry Mathers didn't want trouble. He'd never gotten detention, had never even turned in homework late. But Terry's girlfriend wore jeans and he was sick and tired of hearing Cript make fun of her. That was why he started yelling at Reginald in the hallway between second and third period. A pair of seniors who idolized Cript as someone with the guts to say what others kept to themselves overheard Terry, tackled him, and beat him up.

"You're lucky you got to him first," Cript said as the seniors backed away and one of Terry's friends helped him up to his feet. "I would have clocked him so hard he'd never show his face here again."

Later in the day, a girl yelled down the hallway that Cript was a maniac. Another girl, a junior, spit in the girl's face in retaliation.

At the end of the day, a freshman who couldn't believe someone running for senior class president was seriously suggesting they isolate some of the students by putting barriers around them, told Cript he was a piece of shit.

Cript didn't yell or get angry. He merely turned to the boy, who was three inches shorter and twenty pounds lighter than he was, and said, "You're looking a little dainty yourself. Maybe you should join the girls behind the barriers."

Then he walked away as two juniors, both of whom loved most of what Cript said, backed the freshman against the wall and asked if he'd like to be closed inside his locker.

\*\*\*

Later that day, seeing that Reginald Cript was going to be the Traditonalist pick and that he had a decent chance of winning due to his opponent's incredible unpopularity, another private school let it be known how they felt about the situation. Kaan'Ada Prep School was to the north of United Exceptionalism. They had a long history of being overshadowed by the latter school, but recently Kaan'Ada Prep School had begun to make changes that many of its students loved. The school put an open notice online announcing that any student at United Exceptionalism who didn't want Cript as their senior class president could transfer schools, free of charge.

It sounded like a joke, but it was retweeted so many times by students at United Exceptionalism that it was obvious many underclassman were giving it serious consideration.

# 12

As the final classrooms voted, fewer students bothered showing up to mark a ballot because they believed McMarton and Cript had already won. In Mr. Fornia's class, the largest in United Exceptionalism, six students didn't bother to show up. Of the ones who did, six were rewarded by having their votes lost. Rather than let those students vote again, the school moved forward with the votes it had. McMarton and Cript won that classroom as well.

At the end of the school day, Mr. McHendricks got on the academy public address system and announced that Shelly McMarton and Reginald Cript were the two finalists to become next year's senior class president.

That was also when the first set of hacked emails was released.

*** 

Anna and Yeri weren't particularly enthusiastic about getting online after school that day. They knew what *The Representative* would say, that it was a great day for United Exceptionalism to have someone like Shelly McMarton running for senior class president and that everyone should rally together to ensure Reginald Cript was defeated.

What they didn't expect was to find an email waiting in their inbox from somehow who called himself ParkTheBus. The email had no subject line. The body of the message contained one word: OPEN.

Yeri hesitated in opening the attached file. Since they had started *Notes from the Underground,* he and Anna had been getting constant hate mail and had been on the receiving end of an unceasing barrage of hurtful comments on their blog. Both of them assumed the zipped file was a virus.

"The virus scan doesn't detect anything," Anna said, her eyebrows raised, hopeful.

Yeri said, "Here goes nothing," and clicked on it.

It wasn't a virus. It was a batch of emails that various school officials had sent to each other.

"What are we looking at?" Anna said, wondering why anyone would go to the trouble of secretly emailing them stuff that the faculty at United Exceptionalism had discussed over their official email.

Before Yeri could answer, Anna saw something that made her eyes widen.

"Oh, shit."

***

They immediately posted everything to their blog, then tweeted all of their friends to start reading it and also to send it to everyone else they knew.

In one of the emails, Shelly's faculty advisor, Mr. Podulski, gave talking points to various school administrators on how to marginalize Percy Wethers. Percy was, Mr. Podulski said, to be discounted as hopelessly wishful and unrealistic each time he was mentioned. Any time his name came up in *The Representative*, it should be as an idealistic kid who wanted to give away free stuff, whereas Shelly should be spoken of as the candidate with experience who is able to bring everyone together.

An email from Ms. Yealdon, the journalism teacher, to Chrissy Cassidy, editor of *The Representative*, said to keep referring to Percy's supporters as Percy's Pervs and to continue repeating the idea that Percy and the kids who liked him were all sexist. She also said to make sure the votes of the teachers were included in all tallies of the voting process even though those ballots weren't official until the last classroom had voted. That would be a good way, she said, of letting the students think the race was all but over from the very beginning.

An email from Mrs. Goldenblume, who worked in the academy's front office, told the teachers they should openly support Shelly from day one. She also said that Mr. Podulski would speak to each of them about how they could help Shelly. She also made fun of Percy's faculty advisor as a deluded old hippie.

\*\*\*

Ben and Sarkoff had been waiting in line for twenty minutes to buy tickets to the next Avengers movie. Only ten people were still ahead of them. Neither of them spoke to the other, though, because both were staring at their smart phones and at all the emails *Notes from the Underground* had posted.

"Holy shit," Ben said. "Every single part of the election was skewed."

Sarkoff offered a shrug. "How else did you think someone like Shelly would get elected?"

\*\*\*

The response was not as measured on the wrestling mats, where United Exceptionalism's wrestlers were in the middle of another practice.

"This is exactly why no one trusts a single fucking thing Shelly says or does," the starting 126-pound junior said as he practiced single leg takedowns.

"Why even vote for who we want if the entire process is going to be rigged?" the 220-pound senior said, drilling his fireman's carry. "I mean seriously, just tell us who the senior class president is going to be instead of going through with this charade. It would be a lot less insulting."

The 160-pound state semi-finalist changed levels, shot in for a double leg, then repeated the motion over and over.

"I guaren-fucking-tee this shit doesn't happen at the other schools. Only here."

\*\*\*

On the other side of the county, Cript was reading the emails and laughing so hard he was almost crying. In any other election for senior class president, he would have been soundly defeated. The only reason he was doing well this time was because everyone who voted Traditionalist wanted someone as different from Jorge M. Shrub as possible. The other thing that had vaulted him to popularity was *The Representative* giving him endless free advertising by talking about him every chance they got. If it weren't for those two things, he never would have had a chance at the outset.

While he played aloof and innocent when being questioned on his ideas, he actually knew what he was doing. In short, he was stoking both blind pride in United Exceptionalism and disdain of one segment of its students to rally everyone else together, and the plan was working perfectly.

The icing on the cake was finding out that the one person remaining in his way had only won in the first round of voting, against a complete doofus no less, by rigging the entire process.

"Priceless," Cript said, shaking his head.

It made him so happy he couldn't help but send out a barrage of tweets to everyone he knew, each mocking Shelly.

@TheRealCript, 5:37 pm – Looks like the

pantsuit-wearing version of Jabba the Hut had to cheat to win. Shocker.

@TheRealCript, 6:04 pm — Shaped like a pear AND a cheater? United Exceptionalism deserves better.

*\*\**

Chet Booth read the emails hoping to find something that incriminated Reginald Cript. Surely, the Traditionalist voting had to be rigged like the Reformist voting had been. That was the only explanation for why Booth had lost to a belligerent loudmouth. There was nothing of the sort, however, and Booth finally understood that the students liked an obnoxious and sexist bully more than they liked him. He turned off his computer and bedroom lights and sat in darkness for the rest of the day.

# 13

Winter break lasted two weeks. During the entire vacation, there had been no response from anyone at United Exceptionalism regarding its faculty working to ensure Shelly became the Reformist candidate. Nor had there been a new article from *The Representative*, nothing to confirm or deny the allegations, nothing to deflect attention away. It was simply ignored. Not even Percy Wethers weighed in on the topic. In fact, no one had seen Percy since school had let out two Fridays earlier.

When the students returned after New Years, it was as if the entire ordeal were part of a bad dream. The campus was covered in snow and icicles clung to the tree branches. Blanketed in white, the school looked nothing like it had two weeks earlier. It felt like a different place, with students and teachers alike laughing a little less, each of them realizing what the future of the academy held.

\*\*\*

In the end, the faculty and administration chose not to offer an explanation directly to the students. Instead, they spoke with reporters from *The Representative*, where the questions could be controlled and where they were sure to get out the message they wanted.

Mr. Podulski was quoted as saying, "I understand students' concerns over the legitimacy of the results, but Shelly would have won anyway. The important thing for us now is to find out who leaked those emails so they can be dealt with accordingly."

Ms. Yealdon said, "It's disgusting that someone would try to manipulate the process of electing our senior class president by hacking into our emails and then releasing them to only give a partial account of what was going on."

Mrs. Goldenblume, the front office administrator, said there was a difference between rigging an election and simply trying to sway the results in a certain way.

By lunchtime, Mrs. Goldenblume had resigned from the academy, the only person held the least bit accountable for all that had happened.

\*\*\*

Later the same day, *The Representative* posted their first editorial in two weeks. It began:

*Some students will read the recently released hacked emails and think there was something nefarious about the way we reported*

155

*on the first round of voting for senior class president. The truth is that the school newspaper has always worked toward the betterment of the academy. In this case, that meant endorsing one candidate over another. It's how things work. Furthermore, our reporting of Shelly McMarton and Percy Wethers was always completely fair and unbiased. The important thing now is for the academy to unite around Shelly and ensure Reginald Cript is defeated.*

***

Shelly easily could have denounced Mrs. Goldenblume's role in what had happened. After all, the woman had admitted to playing favorites when she was supposed to be an impartial part of the process. Instead, Shelly went on Facebook and thanked the academy administrator for her hard work and for executing her job in such a professional manner. To show her gratitude, Shelly named Mrs. Goldenblume as an honorary faculty advisor to her campaign.

***

Mr. Podulski called for Shelly to come see him after school. She hadn't managed to enter the classroom or shut the door behind her before he started yelling.

"Are you the most tone deaf student who's ever walked through the academy hallways or just completely stupid?"

"I don't—"

"All you have to do is not be seen or heard and yet you insist on defending Mrs. Goldenblume? You've got to be kidding me." He threw a book across the room. "I want you to be completely honest with me: are you tone deaf or do you simply not care how bad you look in the students' eyes?"

Shelly had been caught off guard when she first walked into her advisor's classroom. In the time it took for

156

Mr. Podulski to blow off steam, she had collected herself.

Considering his question, she stared at him and said, without any emotion at all, "I just don't care what they think of me."

"Well," he said, shaking his head. "At least you've been honest for once in your life."

***

Cript could barely contain himself. All evening, after school let out, he sent out tweets on the subject of the email scandal.

@TheRealCript, 6:30 pm – Percy got played. Pant-suit Shelly is a complete crook. Wow, never seen something so undemocratic.

@TheRealCript, 6:35 pm – All of Percy's supporters should be outraged. Unacceptable what happened. Shelly the Hutt should be ashamed.

@TheRealCript, 6:47 pm – The Reformist elections were completely rigged. Rigged. What a joke.

***

The response on *Notes from the Underground* began:

*The faculty and The Representative both finally released a message today about the leaked emails that showed how the teachers worked to ensure Shelly was the Reformist candidate even before the first vote had been cast. The response was sorely lacking, however, and provided the equivalent of "It stinks that it happened but it's in the past so we should all move forward." The students at United Exceptionalism deserve better. One moment, The Representative says they were clearly providing coverage to endorse Shelly, and then the next moment they say they were providing equally unbiased coverage. Well, which was it? After reading the hacked emails, it's safe to say we all know the answer.*

*As for Percy Wethers, who has ignited a storm of support, we encourage him to run as a write-in candidate. He can still win if everyone who likes what he has to say just writes his name down on Election Day. Maybe in other years that approach wouldn't be feasible, but in a year when the vast majority of students dislike both the Reformist and Traditionalist candidates, anything is possible.*

# 14

In the middle of the night, a new message was posted to Shelly's Facebook page. Considering its general tone and when it was written, most people assumed that it had been written by someone else and posted on her behalf. The message was:

*Thank you, everyone, who voted for me! And thank you to my mother and father for all the support they've shown me. To all of you who worked hard to help me be the Reformist candidate for senior class president, I am truly indebted to you.*

*I also want to thank Percy Wethers for running a great campaign and for inspiring hundreds of students at United Exceptionalism to become more interested in the issues I've been championing since coming to the academy.*

*We must now shift our attention to ensuring Reginald Cript does not become the next senior class president. He seeks to divide us, both from each other and from the rest of the academic world. I will do the opposite. I will be the senior class president for not just the Reformists but for the Traditionalists and everyone in between. Thank you and long live the United Exceptionalism Academy for Boys and Girls!*

***

Not to be outdone, Reginald Cript posted his own message the next day.

*The world is very different now from when our parents went to United Exceptionalism. There are people out there who seek to destroy our academy. We can't afford another senior class president like the one we currently have and that's exactly what Shelly McMarton would be. It will take a lot of work to defeat her. And so, my fellow students: ask not what your academy can do for you, ask what you can do for your academy.*

*I have a dream, a dream where Reformists and Traditionalists come together with me as their senior class president. It will be one small step for school politics, but one giant leap for United Exceptionalism.*

He swore he wrote every word of it himself.

***

At the end of the day, Mr. McHendricks was preparing to address the academy with a couple of important updates. Chet Booth asked if he could say something to the entire student body.

"No cursing," Mr. McHendricks said.

"Of course not."

When he first started speaking, everyone expected him to rally the Traditionalist students together in order to oppose Shelly McMarton. But of course, Chet being Chet, that didn't happen.

"I want to congratulate Reginald Cript on winning the first round of voting and becoming the Traditionalist candidate for senior class president. We live in a world surrounded by evil. Every day, we should be asking ourselves, 'Did we live up to the values we said we believed in?' That's what this election should be about.

Not name-calling or suggestions that someone did or didn't eat a booger that was on his upper lip. Today, we are a divided academy of boys and girls. We have to do better. And so, if you love United Exceptionalism as much as I do, you must... vote your conscience. Thank you, everyone!"

***

Percy didn't show up to school the first two days back from holiday break. No one had seen him or heard from him since the revelation that the Reformist voting in the first round had been engineered to favor Shelly. Because of this, no one was sure how he was going to react.

When he did show up for class later in the week, he was bombarded by kids from every grade asking what he was going to do.

"I'm going to be speaking in the gymnasium during lunch," Percy said with a soft voice. "I'll explain everything then."

Up and down the halls of United Exceptionalism, students speculated about what he might say. Some were sure he was going to run for senior class president as a write-in candidate. Others said he might transfer to another school. Some guessed he would be invited to join Shelly McMarton and have some important responsibilities to help the academy once she became senior class president. In Ms. Yardley's Calculus class, the students were so distracted by talking about what Percy might do that she let everyone out twenty minutes early so they could go to the gym and get a good seat.

When the bell rang, half the school flocked to hear what Percy would say. The janitor had to pull down an extra set of bleachers so everyone had a place to sit. Chants of Percy's name echoed through the cavernous room. When he appeared, everyone stood and applauded.

Others shouted Shelly's name with derision and booed.

After the commotion subsided, Percy said, "Thanks, everyone, we made a lot of progress over the Fall and Winter semesters."

Even this brought about a new round of applause that Percy had to wait for.

"In a short span of time, we were able to take ideas like students wearing flip-flops to class and everyone receiving free laptops and change them from being fringe ideas to realistic possibilities. We got Shelly McMarton to change her stance on a variety of topics, and we upset the status quo. We still have a lot of work to do, though. So, everyone is asking: where do we go from here?"

A girl in the audience yelled, "I'll still write your name down, Percy," and the crowd cheered. Others yelled similar things.

"I'll never vote for Shelly," a couple kids hollered.

Wethers raised his hand for silence.

"We need to focus on defeating Cript. We need to do everything in our power to ensure he doesn't become the next senior class president."

Hundreds of voices began to grumble in confusion.

Percy said, "We need to rally around Shelly McMarton and do everything we can to ensure she becomes the next senior class president, not Cript."

That was when the booing started. The same people had gathered in the gymnasium for weeks to cheer everything Percy said about the average student getting lost in the shuffle of a deck that was monopolized by the alumni's and faculty's wishes. Now, they couldn't believe what they were hearing.

"You said she was everything we should reject," a freshman girl yelled. "And now you want us to support her?"

A freshman boy stood and shouted, "What about getting gypped out of the first round? They screwed you over and you're just going to act like it didn't happen?"

The chorus of boos increased.

"The faculty ripped you off and you're just quitting?" Yeri yelled.

Sitting beside him, all Anna could do was shake her head.

Another student yelled, "I'll never vote for Shelly."

"You're a poser, Percy."

Percy didn't walk out of the gym. He didn't yell for them to be quiet. Instead, he stood there and accepted it all.

When the bleachers quieted down, he said again, "I know how frustrated some of you feel, but the threat of Cript is too great for us not to have a unified voice. I'm sorry."

\*\*\*

After the speech was over, Anna and Yeri remained seated as lines of dejected students filed out of the gym.

"I can't believe that just happened," Anna said.

Yeri kept looking past her, toward the podium, in the hope that Percy would call everyone back and say he had reconsidered.

"A liar no one trusts is going to be facing a sexist pig everyone hates, and the one kid everyone got excited for just accepted it when he got gypped. It's almost like the academy wants to implode. Or, as *The Representative* would say, 'It was a great day in United Exceptionalism's history'."

\*\*\*

On their way out of the gym, some of the senior boys kept saying how badly Percy had gotten screwed over by the administration and were amazed that he was accepting it without a fight.

"Have some dignity, man. Stand up for yourself, you know?"

"If I went after it as hard as Percy did and got fucked over, I'd never just roll over and take it."

The group of seniors kept using one word to characterize Percy. Shawn Trustman, a freshmen, overheard and laughed with them every time they said it, but the truth was that he had no idea what the word meant. He had to sneak away from them to look it up on his phone. The word was "cuckold."

# 15

Over the next week, Shelly went mostly unseen and unheard. Her huge smile faded whenever another student tried to talk to her. The only things she said were that Cript was dangerous and couldn't become senior class president or that the academy needed someone with her background, experience, and level-headedness.

Whenever she was asked about her possible involvement with what had happened in the first round of voting, her smile flickered as she looked for the nearest exit, and then she said she didn't know anything about it.

All attempts by the students to have the elections done over or to count disallowed votes were ignored by United Exceptionalism's administration.

\*\*\*

Percy went back to being as popular as he had been before he decided to run for senior class president, which is to say that most kids didn't pay any attention to him at all. He didn't talk in the gymnasium during lunch. He didn't speak about the dress code or even about the cost of textbooks. When asked about the election, he said he hoped everyone would vote for McMarton and ensure Cript never became senior class president. Other than that, he faded away to become just another face in the crowded hallways of students going to and from their classes.

\*\*\*

Unhappy Reformists weren't the only ones talking about writing in the name of their designated pick. The Traditionalist alumni had never seriously considered the fact that Cript might win the first round of voting. Now that he had, they scrambled for someone who fit the mold of the usual candidates they supported. Ricky Tinsil had thought about running for senior class president before Cript had mocked his overbite and big ears, and the fact that he had one time gotten an F in gym class, which was thought to be impossible. The alumni also thought of Jorge M. Shrub's little brother, but he simply had no ability to hold anyone's attention. He could be telling people that their classroom was on fire and they would still look for something more interesting to listen to. Regardless of whom they chose, the Traditionalist parents were set on Cript not becoming senior class president.

\*\*\*

Cript wasn't concerned by what the alumni thought of him or by Shelly telling everyone he wasn't qualified to be senior class president. He was having too much fun mocking McMarton on Twitter to worry about anything else.

@TheRealCript, 2:41 pm – Can't wait for everyone to find out what a crook Shelly is. I know stuff about her that no one else knows... yet.

@TheRealCript, 4:34 pm – This academy needs a leader, not a pear-shaped liar that no one likes. #ShittyShelly

@TheRealCript, 5:11 pm – Shelly isn't going to be able to rig the next round like she rigged the first round. Loser.

\*\*\*

In a way, Chet Booth became more popular after the first round of voting. Everywhere he went, students had something they wanted to say to him. It was never anything positive, though.

"Maybe you understand now why no one likes you, huh?" a senior girl said.

"You've got to be the most bitter, most selfish piece of shit I've ever seen," a junior boy said.

A sophomore said, "I always told my friends that there was no way you could become even more hated than after you tried to get the school dance cancelled. You definitely proved me wrong."

Each time a student said something like this to him, Chet would smile and say he loved United Exceptionalism and just wanted it to be an academy everyone could be proud of.

"I'll be proud of this place if you start going to a different school," a girl said, then walked in the direction of her history class before the final bell rang.

\*\*\*

After school that day, Anna and Yeri held hands as they walked around their neighborhood. All around them were cardinals and blue jays chirping as if the world was full of things to sing about. Each happy call made Anna fidget until Yeri shook her hand and told her to relax.

"Everything will be okay."

She looked at him in astonishment. "How can you say that?"

He smiled and motioned at the beautiful homes and at the trees that were beginning to get leaves again, at the flowers that would soon bloom and grace the sidewalks with every possible color.

"So we won't have a senior class president we like, what's the worst that could happen?"

It had been a rhetorical question. She was supposed to hear it and understand that in the greater scheme of things, they both had their health, their families, and each other. That was all they truly needed. Anna couldn't help herself, though.

"What's the worst that could happen? Another school gets a visit from our football team and barely lives to tell about it, the academy continues to deteriorate while the faculty focus on nonsense, kids keep getting sick from drinking at tainted water fountains, and the next senior class president does whatever the alumni want rather than what's best for the students."

"Oh."

# Spring Semester

# 1

There was only a one-week break between the winter and spring semesters, but to the students who were following the race for senior class president, it felt completely different. For the most part, Percy and Chet had disappeared. Two other students, a pair almost no one liked, were now the official Reformist and Traditionalist candidates. No one saw or heard much from Shelly McMarton. Cript, on the other hand, seemed to be everywhere.

\*\*\*

The strangest thing, at least to Yeri and Anna, was that no one was talking about all the things that had happened in the first round of Reformist voting to benefit Shelly. Both kids had hoped to come back to school and hear that the voting would be done all over again. Maybe Shelly would be automatically disqualified and Percy would be declared the winner. At the very least, there would be a protest or a sit-in. What they saw, however, was that no one even seemed to remember it had happened.

Their friends shrugged as if it was old news, then uttered some variation of the sentiment, "The choice for United Exceptionalism is now between 'Bad' and 'Worse'."

Mr. Blathon, the Music teacher, said, "The students have spoken and they've decided the next senior class president will either be McMarton or Cript."

"They didn't decide," Anna grumbled to Yeri. "It was rigged."

She wanted to yell it from the roof of United Exceptionalism but knew it was pointless. Mr. Blathon was only one of the teachers at the academy. None of the others were complaining about what had happened either.

Mr. Podulski told *The Representative*, "Shelly has a tough challenge ahead of her but I'm confident she can rally the school to come together and defeat that boy running as the Traditionalist candidate. Quite frankly, I've never seen such a frightful option for senior class president as the Traditionalists are offering this year. Whatever we do, we need to make sure Shelly is elected and he isn't."

\*\*\*

Soon after, Yeri and Anna asked Mr. Podulski if he wouldn't mind being interviewed for *Notes from the Underground*. Anna was determined to hold someone accountable for what had happened in the first round of voting.

"If Shelly needed the first round of voting to be heavily swayed in her favor in order to win, are you at all concerned that she might actually lose against Cript?"

Mr. Podulski's eyes narrowed. The little bit of humor that had been on his face vanished. Anna thought he might argue the point and say it hadn't been rigged.

Instead, with a complete lack of emotion on his face, he said, "No, and it looks like that will have to be the last question." He gestured at a stack of papers that had seemed unimportant earlier when she asked if he had time to talk. "A lot of papers to grade, you know?"

"We only got to ask one question," Yeri said.

Mr. Podulski didn't bother looking up from the paper he was already pretending to grade. "That is correct."

\*\*\*

In a sign that he was either learning the game or that the Traditionalists realized they were stuck with him and should try to help him out, Cript finally got a faculty advisor of his own.

"You'll help me get elected?" he asked Ms. Sales, a math teacher.

"That's what I'm here for. Each candidate gets one. You were supposed to have one in the first round as well."

"Ha!" Cript said, his hair flopping as he laughed. "Who knew?"

\*\*\*

Yeri went to talk to Ms. Sales the next day to ask her most of the same questions about the race for senior class president that Anna had planned to ask Mr. Podulski.

"Don't ask me," Ms. Sales said.

"Aren't you his faculty advisor?"

"I was—for a day. He didn't like my advice so he fired me. Said he knew what was best."

Yeri asked if Cript was planning to get a different advisor.

The math teacher's mouth curled in at one side the way it did when a student let her down. "Beats me. Who knows what that kid'll say or do next?"

\*\*\*

None of the attention was on Cript the next day, however, because that was when the next McMarton email scandal broke out.

# 2

Shelly's parents had started a charity in her name, mostly as a tax write-off for themselves, but also as a way to get the academy's alumni and faculty invested in their daughter from an early age. Many parents at United Exceptionalism did the same thing because they were wealthy enough to understand the benefits of the tax breaks they were afforded by setting up such an arrangement.

Shelly's charity was regarded as one of the most successful at the school, with local business leaders and alumni contributing large sums of money for whatever she wanted to do with it. Most kids used their personal email to collect money. Only Shelly thought it was a good idea to use a general email account associated with United Exceptionalism to collect money on her charity's behalf.

Of course, this was forbidden by the academy's rules. A year earlier, Trevor Gallagher, a junior at United Exceptionalism who had never gotten in any trouble before, was expelled from the academy for using the official academy email system in order to send out online invitations to his birthday party. Trevor had broken the rules one time. Shelly, it turned out, had used United Exceptionalism's official email server for over a year.

It only came to light because someone working in the principal's office had forwarded the emails to *The Representative, Notes from the Underground,* and a variety of faculty and alumni.

\*\*\*

As with everything else involving the race for

senior class president, the revelation of the emails elicited drastically different reactions.

The Reformists who support Shelly cried that there was a witch hunt going on and that McMarton was just trying to do something good. However, only a third of the students were Reformists and only half of them supported Shelly. Everyone else wished varying degrees of misfortune upon her. The Reformists who had supported Percy Wethers saw this as karma. They also held out an irrational hope that this would somehow lead to Shelly's expulsion and Percy replacing her as the official Reformist candidate.

The students who were neither Reformist nor Traditionalist saw a girl who had always come off as being pompous and dishonest and were glad that she had finally gotten what was coming to her.

It was no surprise that the strongest reaction came from the Traditionalists. A pair of Traditionalist alumni who had been tracking Shelly's ambitions since she was a freshman, clanged glasses and toasted her demise.

"We finally got her," one said with a smile.

"The wicked witch is dead," the other said and downed his wine in two large gulps.

\*\*\*

United Exceptionalism didn't take immediate disciplinary action against Shelly. Instead, they said they would perform an official investigation into what had happened.

When Trevor Gallagher heard this, he said to his friends, "I wish I would have been special enough to get an official investigation. They didn't waste any time in expelling my dumb ass."

\*\*\*

Having beaten the only candidate who actually had more students like him than dislike him, Shelly was now considered a shoo-in to become senior class president. After all, no one in their right mind would vote for Reginald Cript after he singled out a portion of the student body and characterized them as sluts and whores.

That was why *The Representative* felt comfortable posting an article that began:

*Shelly McMarton's use of official United Exceptionalism email for personal gain shows an alarming lack of judgment...*

Although that same article ended with the pronouncement:

*...And that's why Shelly will learn from this mistake and go on to become the greatest senior class president this academy has known.*

\*\*\*

Cript saw how much everyone despised Shelly and couldn't help himself. Instead of leaving well enough alone, he had to join in.

@TheRealCript, 6:39 pm – Turns out that lying skank Shelly isn't only a cheater, she's also a completely unethical con artist. Wow.

@TheRealCript, 7:25 pm – A new low point in this academy's history. Shelly McMarton has disqualified herself by using school email for her personal charity. Crook.

@TheRealCript, 7:41 pm – Why hasn't someone thrown Shelly down a flight of stairs yet? Maybe because the stairs don't deserve that kind of treatment.

The Faulty Process of Electing a Senior Class President

*** 

At the same time, Chrissy Cassidy posted an editorial that began:

*Reginald Cript's recent retweet of a sexist meme disqualifies him from being our next senior class president. He should immediately quit his campaign. This academy's only hope for a safe and secure future is Shelly McMarton, whose devotion to this academy cannot be questioned and who would never retweet something making fun of any segment of the student body.*

# 3

With the help of his second faculty advisor, Cript turned his campaign up a level. And that wasn't a good thing. The second teacher he selected to help him navigate the treacherous path to becoming senior class president played to all of Reginald's worst traits.

Susie Mecklandowski was one of the newest teachers at United Exceptionalism. In the five years since graduating college, she had taught at two other private schools. She saw in Cript a way to elevate herself. Almost no one took Cript seriously even though he was the official Traditionalist candidate. Mecklandowski was sure that if she could get him elected senior class president, she would become one of the most notable faculty members at the academy and someone the rich alumni looked to for advice.

Mecklandowski had been following Cript's misadventures since the boy had first announced his interest in becoming the next senior class president. In that time, she had come to realize that the same things that would kill other campaigns were the very things that made Reginald's supporters like him. She also saw that Cript struggled whenever he tried to be more like a typical senior class president candidate. That was why she suggested he never moderate what he said or did. Quite the opposite, he should be as outrageous as he liked.

She expected this to be taken as good news. Instead, after explaining it to Reginald, the boy's response was, "What do I need you for then? I don't need a faculty member to tell me to keep being myself. I know what I'm doing. I don't even know what I'm doing and I've gotten this far."

Mecklandowski, seeing her time as Cript's faculty advisor coming to as rapid an end as Ms. Sales's, jumped into action.

"I'll do your dirty work for you. If any of Shelly's people get in your way, I'll handle it. If any of the faculty take issue with something you say or do, I'll clear it up."

Cript stared at the woman—twice his age and a paid academy faculty member—as if she were an employee.

Stone-faced, Cript asked, "Would you kill someone if I asked you to?"

Mecklandowski's heart skipped a beat. Her throat contracted, making it impossible to swallow.

"I'm just kidding," Cript said, his face breaking into a large, devilish grin. "But not really." Mecklandowski's face tried to form into a smile. "But yeah, I'm joking. Or not."

\*\*\*

With a member of United Exceptionalism's

faculty squarely behind him, Cript took the academy by storm.

The starting point guard on the basketball team bumped shoulders with Cript in the hallway and muttered, "Sexist asshole."

Cript didn't think twice. He raised his voice and called out, "Someone beat this prick up. First guy that does gets a new iPhone and I'll pay for any legal fees you have."

Unfortunately for the point guard, Luke Basquet was nearby. Luke was known for taking any dare he was offered. On one occasion, he urinated in his own hand for a dollar. He swallowed a lit cigarette for five dollars. Being offered the latest model of smartphone just to beat up some jock? It was a no-brainer as far as Luke was concerned.

\*\*\*

Yeri saw the kid get beat up in the hallway and mentioned it on *Notes from the Underground*, emphasizing what Reginald had said to prompt the beating. What he realized, though, was that it somehow didn't seem like that big of a deal. Months earlier it would have. But months earlier there also hadn't been a boy calling for the isolation of a segment of the student body, a kid actually suggesting that walls be built around girls he considered to be promiscuous. In the time since, everyone had seen Cript's antics and had been shocked by the things he had said and done. Compared to all of that, a basketball player getting beat up didn't seem like news.

\*\*\*

*The Representative* sent another reporter to do an interview with Cript. The school paper had been running pieces nonstop about him since the beginning of the school year because they were always the most widely read articles. In the Spring semester, however, the articles and editorials began to take on a decidedly negative tone. Whereas Cript had once been portrayed as an off-the-cuff candidate, not thinking before he spoke but nonetheless entertaining, he was now referred to as a hate-filled boy, a sexist, a young tyrant, and a potential disaster for United Exceptionalism if he became senior class president.

It didn't take long for Cript's patience with the paper to wear thin. Only a couple days into the semester, he lost his temper with the sophomore reporter sent to interview him.

"Is this gonna be another hack job?" He asked before the girl could ask a single question.

Tonya Dellatone, a girl who knew she was going to become a world famous writer one day, looked up from her notes.

"Huh?"

"I said," Cript repeated, speaking painfully slowly and exaggerating the words as if speaking to a simpleton, "is... this... going... to... be... another... hack... job?"

"Uh, I don't know what happened with the other kids who covered you for *The Representative*, I'm just here to ask you some questions and—"

"I'm just here to ask you some questions," Cript mimicked, his hands flailing.

He waited for Tonya to say something, anything. When she didn't, he sighed, tapping his foot against the floor and his knuckles against the wall.

When she still didn't speak, he said, "You know what? Get the fuck out. I'm done talking to you. What a colossal waste of my time. Go fuck yourself."

Tonya stared at Cript, completely caught off guard. Some of her friends, both boys and girls, loved to gossip and surround themselves with drama. It was common of kids her age. But Tonya wasn't like that. She never raised her voice. She never treated the students around her in any way other than how she would want to be treated. So when Cript yelled at her, it didn't upset her as much as it confounded her.

"What did I say?"

"Did I stutter? Get the fuck out!"

Tonya looked around. "We're in the library."

Reginald's eyes narrowed. She could see from his expression that he had forgotten this was the first time he had agreed to be interviewed someplace other than his family's mansion.

Looking around and seeing only one other student nearby, he said, "Fine, whatever," and stood up. He was ten feet toward the library doors when he turned and added, "I hope you get pregnant the very first time you have sex—if you can find a boy desperate enough to do it to you."

Then he left the library, laughing at how he had successfully dealt with the situation.

*** 

What Cript didn't know yet, and Ms. Mecklandowski was only just now hearing whispers of, was that the Traditionalist alumni and faculty were so concerned with Cript being their candidate that they were thinking of ways to get him removed. Whoever else they picked would surely lose but it was better, in their eyes, than actually having Cript be senior class president. There were also rumors they were so disgruntled they were considering throwing their support behind McMarton, something that would have been unimaginable only months earlier.

Suddenly, the impossible was possible. And that wasn't always a good thing.

# 4

Everyone at United Exceptionalism knew the email scandal was serious when the principal appointed a faculty member to perform a special investigation. Jim Comb, Head of Student Security, had a reputation for playing by the book. He didn't care if a student was a freshman or a senior, a Reformist or Traditionalist, or who their parents happened to be. Each kid was treated the same way, which meant they were left alone as long as they followed the academy's strict code of conduct. When they didn't, they had a meeting with Comb.

However, if the faculty and students were hoping for a quick resolution to the clear violations Shelly McMarton had committed, they were sorely mistaken. Comb's investigation wouldn't be completed in a day or even a week.

When asked how long it would take, he said, "As long as it takes."

When asked if it might take so long that the election for senior class president could have already occurred, he said, "That's certainly possible."

*** 

Comb started by reviewing the email accounts McMarton had used. What he found was that there weren't dozens of emails, as he had expected, but hundreds. Shelly had been using United Exceptionalism's official email accounts for even longer than she had admitted.

As he scanned through the emails, something else became abundantly clear. He found responses to emails that hadn't been received, at least as far as the inbox said.

He also found emails referencing other messages that weren't there.

Someone had intentionally deleted hundreds of emails.

***

"I'd like to speak to Shelly about the emails," Comb said to Shelly's mother as he stood on the welcome mat outside their house.

"And I'd like to be twenty years younger," Mrs. McMarton said. "Good luck with that."

"Is that a no?"

Mrs. McMarton took a deep drag off the cigarette that was perched at the end of her lips. A moment later, the smoke billowed out from her nostrils like two smokestacks sending smog into the atmosphere.

"Ask her lawyer if that means no."

Then she closed the front door.

***

Comb's next step was to interview the senior who had set up the email accounts and had also given Shelly password access to them.

The boy, Pat Snowers, put a hand in the air after Comb's first question.

"I'm not saying anything unless I get a letter, in writing, that says I won't be held accountable for anything that happened."

"You want to be given immunity?" Comb said, shaking his head that a teenage boy would even think to ask for such a thing."

"Yeah, immunity. That's what I want. Or I'm not talking."

***

Comb went back to Pat Snowers the next day with a signed letter on official United Exceptionalism letterhead that said the senior wouldn't be held accountable for any wrongdoing and that no matter what he had done in regards to the email system, he wouldn't even get so much as a single day's detention. Pat looked the paper over, then nodded.

"Okay," Comb said. "Then let's get started." He pulled out a pad of paper and clicked his pen. "Tell me exactly what you did for Shelly regarding the email access."

Pat gave a playful smile. "I'm going to invoke the fifth."

"The fifth?" Comb's voice rose. He could barely contain the frustration. "The fifth? What do you think this is? We're talking about the academy's email system, not felonies."

"Yeah, either way, I'm not going to answer any questions."

"Why on earth did you have me sign that paper for you then?" he asked, nodding toward the sheet that guaranteed the boy immunity.

"Someone's head is gonna roll for what happened. And it sure as hell ain't gonna be Shelly's. I wanted to make sure it wasn't mine either."

\*\*\*

Although hundreds of emails had been deleted, Comb began to read the ones that were still there. Most were nothing more than Shelly emailing alumni about her charity and asking for donations, but some were to other students and also to faculty members. He went and spoke to these people next.

Most didn't recall any emails. Even when he slid a printed copy of the chain of messages across the table for them to review, students and faculty alike commonly said they didn't remember sending or receiving anything like that. Only a few admitted they had.

"Did you ever talk to Shelly about the use of official school email for her private use?"

"I mentioned it one time," a senior named Whitney Gaunt said.

"What was Shelly's response?"

"I think her exact response was, 'Never mention it again'."

\*\*\*

*The Representative* posted an article about the email scandal. Somehow, even though Shelly refused to speak about it with Comb or anyone else, the school paper had managed to find multiple sources who agreed to talk. All spoke on the condition of anonymity, but said Shelly had only used the academy's email system in that manner because a boy who had already graduated told her he had done the same thing.

They did not pose the obvious next question, which was whether or not Shelly would have jumped off a cliff just because an upperclassman had told her he had done that as well.

\*\*\*

Comb found out which college that boy was attending and gave him a call.

"Is it true you told Shelly McMarton to use the academy's official email system for personal gain because you had done the same thing yourself?"

The boy laughed. Then, realizing Comb was serious, scoffed and said, "That's bullshit. I told her not to use the email system that way. Not to!"

# 5

When Cript wasn't sending out tweets criticizing McMarton or retweeting derogatory messages posted by other kids, he was walking around the halls of United Exceptionalism telling every student who would listen that the academy needed someone strong and trustworthy like him instead of "some dishonest and manipulative wench" like McMarton.

When asked by a freshman if he realized it was sexist and insulting to speak of Shelly in that manner, he asked the girl if it was her time of the month.

***

A group of sophomore boys were at a table next to one where Cript was laughing with some junior girls. One of the boys, a short kid with oily hair nicknamed The Rooster, said he couldn't wait until next year when Cript's little sister started going to United Exceptionalism. As the boy put it, he would "want to get some of that."

Reginald overheard this and stood from the table where he had been talking to the girls. The rest of the sophomore boys went quiet. The two on either side of The Rooster scooted away from him so they weren't associated with anything he had said. The last thing these boys wanted was Cript's bull's-eye to fall on them like it had on the starting point guard who had received a thrashing in the hallway.

Reginald walked the ten feet over to the next table and put a hand on The Rooster's shoulder. The kid's face turned red. His crowing laugh, which had been the reason for his nickname, became an awkward squawk.

Reginald didn't hit the kid, though. Nor did he call on any of his nearby supporters to do his dirty work for him.

Instead, he smiled and said, "I don't blame you. I mean, she *is* super hot. Way too sexy for someone like you, though."

Then he walked away and began joking around with another table of kids.

\*\*\*

The first poll of the spring semester came out and showed something truly remarkable. When asked to describe Reginald Cript in a single word, the most common responses were: Sexist, Stupid, Bigoted, Egotistical, and Ignorant.

When asked who they would vote for between Shelly McMarton and Reginald Cript, 52% of those same students said they would vote for him. Half of them said they liked at least one of the ideas he was talking about implementing as senior class president. The other half simply despised Shelly McMarton and said they would never vote for her.

\*\*\*

That evening, Wade Copper, the Statistics teacher and the man whose analysis of student polling was almost always accurate, wrote a piece for *The Representative* that said the first student poll should be ignored.

"Polls this time of year are pointless and unreliable," he wrote. "Wait another couple weeks before expecting to see polls with reliable results."

At the same time, he indicated there was an eighty-two percent chance Shelly McMarton would become the next senior class president. However, he didn't give quantifiable evidence for this prediction other than what his gut told him.

Anna read the piece and turned to Yeri. "Maybe they should have asked the Philosophy teacher for concrete numbers to back up the claim."

***

Scott Eubanks, a senior and the starting shortstop on the baseball team, saw Cript talking to a pair of sophomore girls and called out, "Neither of them is as hot as your sister, right?"

Cript appraised both girls from head to toe and then winked and said, "Not even close."

Each time he said something like this, the other kids laughed as if it was all good fun and an obvious joke even though Reginald insisted it wasn't.

Maybe it was the way he smiled while he said it. Maybe it was the way he seemed habitually distracted. Whatever the reason, he saw the reaction he got and he continued to play along. He could say anything he wanted and the kids who already hated him would still hate him. They didn't matter, though. The kids who liked him, and there were many who did, would respect him even more each time he said something that no one else would dare say.

# 6

The following week, Comb happened to pass Shelly in one of the hallways.

"You didn't happen to change your mind about talking to me, did you?"

Her response was to look the other way and keep walking.

\*\*\*

Comb didn't know everything there was to know because most people refused to talk to him. But what he had gathered was troubling. Shelly hadn't just used United Exceptionalism's email system for something other than official academy correspondence, she had used it for personal financial gain. And she hadn't only done so once or twice or even for one month or two months but for a year and a half. Added to that was her refusal to cooperate with his investigation and the fact that someone had deleted hundreds of emails she had sent and received.

By itself, that would be enough for him to recommend she be expelled from the academy.

\*\*\*

Charity Ferguson was only a freshman at United Exceptionalism but she knew someone important had entered the principal's office. When a middle-aged man with silver hair and a gray suit walked past the reception desk where Charity was helping, she took note. When that man walked directly into the Director of Student Affairs office without knocking or even asking if the woman was busy, Charity knew she had seen someone of note.

She looked over at William Lee, a boy who was one year ahead of her and constantly flirting with her.

Before she could ask the question, William whispered, "Mr. McMarton. Shelly's dad."

\*\*\*

Charity told her best friend about what she had seen—the father of the likely next senior class president, walking into the office of Lorraine Staunch, the woman who just happened to be the boss of the man investigating Shelly's use of email. That girl told her boyfriend. Her boyfriend told Yeri. Yeri, of course, didn't waste any time telling Anna and also posting about it on *Notes from the Underground.*

The story spread like wildfire. Kids were tweeting it and retweeting it. It was the most commonly discussed topic on *The Representative's* discussion boards even though no one from the official school paper had reported on it or confirmed what had happened.

\*\*\*

When Lorraine Staunch arrived to school the next day, a group of people wanted to speak with her. Among them were a reporter from *The Representative*, both Anna and Yeri, Shelly's faculty advisor, and, maybe most important, Jim Comb himself.

One person who didn't want to speak with the Director of Student Affairs was the principal.

"I don't want to know what's going on; keep me out of this," he shouted as he walked past them and closed the door to his office.

The girl from the school paper asked Lorraine if it was true she had met with Shelly McMarton's father.

Anna asked a better question: "Ms. Staunch, why

did you decide to meet with Shelly's father while Mr. Comb is investigating his daughter?"

Yeri smiled. Not only didn't it give the Director a chance to deny the meeting had happened, it also acknowledged the blazingly clear conflict of interest in holding the meeting.

Lorraine smiled at everyone gathered around her. Instinctually, without even realizing she was doing it, her eyes darted to each corner of the ceiling. She was looking for cameras—the act of someone who might be caught doing something improper. It was useless to deny the meeting, though, and she knew it. In the age of cell phones, anyone in the principal's office could have snapped a picture of Shelly's father walking into her office like the buffoon he was. Better to acknowledge it and minimize the whole thing.

"We're old friends," she said with a smile. "He happened to be driving past the academy yesterday and just wanted to stop in and say hello."

Yeri snickered, waiting for her real answer. When Comb, Staunch, and everyone else looked at him, not a single muscle moving on any of their faces, he realized Lorraine hadn't been joking; that was her actual excuse.

\*\*\*

Later that morning, *The Representative* posted an article about the meeting between Shelly's father and the Director of Student Affairs. The piece had multiple quotes from Lorraine. One had her admitting the meeting could certainly look suspicious but that it was purely coincidental, a meeting of friends. Another quote had her saying that the meeting with Shelly's father would in no way influence Jim Comb's investigation.

Of course, only a couple hours later, Comb finished his investigation and suggested that Shelly not only be allowed to continue attending classes at United

Exceptionalism, but that she receive no punishment at all.

Not even ten minutes passed before Lorraine Staunch issued a statement saying she accepted Comb's recommendation.

\*\*\*

@TheRealCript, 3:31 pm – Did anyone actually think Shelly was going to get expelled? What a sham.

@TheRealCript, 4:10 pm – Looks like Shelly can get away with whatever she wants. #Untouchable. #Rigged.

\*\*\*

The following day, Comb went onto *The Representative*'s main website and created a post about why he had recommended Shelly receive no punishment at all. This is what he said:

*As you all know, I was recently tasked with investigating a student's use of United Exceptionalism's private email system for her possible personal gain. I'm here to give you my reasoning for why I suggested no disciplinary action be brought against that student. I'm doing this because I think the students at this academy deserve to know what happened.*

*My investigation looked at whether there was evidence that United Exceptionalism's email system was improperly used in accordance with academy conduct guidelines. During my investigation, I read approximately 3,000 emails sent or received by the student via the academy's email system. I also estimate that roughly 300 additional emails were deleted without my being able to read them. I also conducted interviews with people who were involved. At no point during the investigation was the student or anyone tied to the student helpful in answering my questions. In fact, all of them were flatly uncooperative.*

*What did my investigation find? Clear evidence that the student intended to use the email system for personal gain, that she did so for more than one academic year, and that part of what was discussed was intentionally concealed. It is obvious that someone in this student's position would have known this was improper.*

*Although there is evidence of potential violations of United Exceptionalism's regulations, it is my judgment that there was no intent to break the rules. Rules were broken and the student should have known better, but I did not see an effort to knowingly and willfully act against the academy's code of conduct.*

*This is not to suggest that in similar circumstances, a student at United Exceptionalism who engaged in the exact same activity would face no consequences. Quite the opposite. They would most likely be expelled.*

***

Chip Myers had been suspended from United Exceptionalism for one week for bringing a samurai sword into class as part of his project on Japanese history. He had no idea the antique would bring the wrong kind of attention and yet he had been sent home for five days.

His response, upon reading Comb's message, was, "You've got to be shitting me!"

***

Marcus Shellanbonnus had been expelled from United Exceptionalism during his junior year for accidentally bringing his brother's stash of Oxycodone to school instead of his own prescription of Ritalin—both of which were in unmarked containers. A year later, he still kept in touch with his old friends from the academy. His reaction to Comb's message was limited to three words.

"W-H-A-T T-H-E F-U-C-K!"

***

"I don't understand," Anna said.

Yeri put his arm around her. "I don't either."

"No, I mean, I really don't get it. He's admitting that Shelly broke the academy rules for over a year, had to know she was doing something wrong, either deleted hundreds of emails herself or had someone else do it, and—and!—admits that if any other kid did it they'd get in trouble, and yet he's recommending no punishment?"

Yeri sighed. It was one of those times in life—and there would be many of them as he got older—in which he saw someone he loved being engulfed in unhappiness and felt helpless to do anything about it.

All he could say was, "It's a messed up academy we go to."

# 7

Shelly wasn't the only one with a charity. Reginald Cript had one as well. His had also been set up by his parents for tax reasons, although he couldn't actually explain what his charity did or what its purpose was.

"I do so much good," he told anybody who would listen. "We've donated thousands of dollars to various causes. Thousands. You name it, we've done it. I'm so proud of what my charity does. It's the best."

\*\*\*

There wasn't anything Reginald could say that would turn off the students who liked him. One of his most cringe-worthy moments came when he said a boy on the track and field team was a loser for breaking his back and becoming paralyzed in a fluke pole-vaulting accident. ("I prefer kids who win, you know? Kids who don't cripple themselves.") He also bragged he could murder another student and not get expelled.

A month into the spring semester, he sought out controversy again. He was walking from one lunch table to another, laughing with the students about Shelly McMarton and what an awful person she was.

"I don't know what can be done about her. She's kind of untouchable, you know? The academy will never allow her to get in trouble, that's for sure. I guess maybe if a group of students goes hunting in the woods and she happens to be out there, somebody could finally stop her. I don't know."

Sophomore Ridley Purencross's face crinkled disapprovingly. She didn't like Shelly and thought she was conniving and dishonest, but Cript made her skin crawl. She could see his war on girls in jeans expanding into a war on cheerleaders or any other nonsensical notion that crossed his mind.

"You're saying someone should shoot her?" There was unmistakable disgust in her tone.

Cript put his hands out in front of him, fending off the accusation. "I'm not saying that at all." He turned and winked at a table of kids next to him. "I'm just saying maybe if she happened to be out in the woods, someone might mistake her for a deer or something."

***

*The Representative* sent Brian Toppert to interview Reginald because Cript had already blacklisted Betsy and two other girls. This interview, like most of the others, would take place at Reginald's house rather than at school.

Brian looked around at the entryway and the

paintings and whistled. The marble floors and columns had what looked to be hand-carved designs and probably cost as much as Brian's car. Cript clapped Brian on the back as if they were old pals and ushered him to the nearby sofas. Brian got right down to business.

"Yesterday, you said someone should kill Shelly, is that right?"

Cript laughed the question away. To him, even though he had never spoken to Brian before, they were both boys and that made them part of the same fraternity.

"No, I just said she's pretty untouchable, you know? The email scandal proved that. If any other kid did that they'd be out of United Exceptionalism and on their ass faster than you could say 'scumbag.' But not her."

Brian looked down at his notes, and then read from one of the pages. "What you said was, 'I guess maybe if a group of students is hunting in the woods and'—"

"I didn't say that."

Brian frowned and looked down at a note he had scribbled, then said, "I have video of it if you'd like—"

"I know what I said, all right? I don't need you to tell me what I said. You're just taking stuff out of context because that's what the school paper does."

Brian shrugged and moved on. "Okay, so there's a video of you from last year saying you supported Jorge M. Shrub sending the football team to Iroquois Regional High School to rough up the kids there, yet now you say you were never in favor of it. Which is it?"

The last vestiges of Cript's smile vanished. He stared at Brian and took a deep breath.

"Next."

"You don't want to answer—"

"Next."

"Okay, sure. So, as you know, every student running for senior class president releases a copy of their transcripts so the other students can see what kind of grades they're getting. Shelly has said she'll release hers but you keep saying you won't release yours. Why?"

"They're complicated."

"Your grades are complicated?"

"Yeah, sure. Listen, I take a lot of classes. I have an independent study. I don't have a normal set of transcripts or else I'd release them. But I'll release them at the end of the year, after the academy has finished their review of them."

"What about last year's transcript?"

"Same thing."

"Your freshman transcripts?"

"Nope."

Brian frowned and looked up from his notes. Cript had his arms folded in defiance.

"How are the students supposed to know what kind of grades you get?"

"Because I've told them. I do wonderful in all my classes."

"Then why not release your—"

"I can see how this is going to be. I thought it might be different since you don't have a vagina—or maybe you do, I don't know. But it's obvious all you people from *The Representative* have it in for me. The school newspaper might as well ask Shelly to be its prom date. Bunch of losers."

"I'm just asking questions students should know the answers to."

"No. You know what you're doing? You're wasting my time. I could be doing anything I want right now and for some reason I'm sitting here wasting it by talking to a hack reporter."

The veins in Brian's neck pulsated with irritation. He thought to tell Cript he didn't actually have a chance of winning the election and that two thirds of the academy thought he was the punch line to a joke. Instead, he decided not to let Reginald know his words had bothered him. He did this by rolling his eyes and walking out of

Cript's mansion without saying another word.

On Brian's way across the driveway to his car, Cript yelled from the house, "And if you post even one untrue thing about me in that loser paper of yours, I'll have my dad sue the shit out of you."

\*\*\*

Cript was still unaware about the lengths that the alumni at United Exceptionalism would go to in order to stop him. Cript's faculty advisor knew but realized that wasn't the type of thing Reginald would want to hear.

Once or twice a week, either at the most expensive restaurant in town or at the country club, a group of four wealthy alumni would meet and discuss how to handle Cript. The men had an enormous amount of influence on the election's outcome, primarily in the form of the money they provided to make campaign banners that hung around every hallway and building. As much as candidates liked to think it was their ideas that won elections, and occasionally it was, it was usually just the kid with the most banners around the academy who won. Name recognition was everything.

"That boy's a moron and a bastard," one said of Reginald.

"And a liability," another added. "He's not just going to lose the election, he's going to destroy the Traditionalists."

All four men wore suits from the time they got out of bed to the time they returned home at night. Each puffed a cigar while speaking.

"No student is going to take the Traditionalists seriously if Reginald is our candidate. The freshmen are going to take one look at him and never vote for another Traditionalist. And you know what? I wouldn't blame them."

"He already won the first round of voting. What

can we do?"

The man seated at the middle of the table, silent until then, inhaled and said, "I'd disown my son if he ever asked Shelly out on a date. I'd rather he be gay than even think she was pretty, let alone have a crush on her. She's the reason they had the Salem witch trials. She's the reason I can still get along with my first wife—because no one else seems quite so bad compared to that girl. But I'll tell you something: she's a known commodity. We can play ball with her. Donate money to her charity and she'll renew your contract to do all the plumbing and electric at United Exceptionalism. Write her a check and she'll make sure your company keeps the vending rights at the academy. There's no telling what that dumbass Reginald will do. That's what frightens me."

"What do we do then?"

The men each smoked their cigars while they thought about the answer. The options were clear. They could support the Traditionalist candidate even though they would be betting on a losing horse and even though he would ruin the reputation of all Traditionalists. That was out. They could support his opposition even though they despised her and it went against everything they believed in. Or they could sit out this year's election for senior class president and begin thinking about the next year's election.

# 8

Following Comb's investigation, Shelly was rarely seen. She was never in homeroom or her normal classes. When *The Representative* asked for interviews, they were referred to Mr. Podulski or one of the other faculty members who supported her.

Eventually, this message was posted to her Facebook page:

*I'm happy but not surprised that Jim Comb finished his investigation and found that I did nothing wrong. I'm also glad he acknowledged that I was honest and cooperative during each step of the process. We can now forget about this and focus on defeating Reginald Cript.*

\*\*\*

"You've got to be kidding me," Anna said, shaking her head. "Comb literally said the exact opposite of what Shelly's claiming."

Yeri sighed. "Orwell is either rolling over in his grave or laughing at the insanity of it all."

\*\*\*

Ever since the first round of voting finished, Melissa and Rachel shifted their focus from attacking Percy Wethers to crying out with indignation that Reginald Cript was a sexist bigot. They still used roughly twenty different fake accounts to post their brand of propaganda. More and more of their time was spent at *Notes from the Underground.* Even though Anna and Yeri's website posted an equal amount of negative stories about Cript and McMarton, even one article criticizing Shelly was too many. After the next blog post there, in which Comb's statement was compared against Shelly's and all the differences highlighted, the two girls knew they had to jump into action.

Shelly-4-Life posted: *This blog obviously hates McMarton. They have a problem with everything she says. Not sure why anyone would bother coming here if they want impartial reporting.*

True Belieber posted: *Comb said she did nothing wrong and chose not to recommend any punishment, yet when Shelly confirms this she's the evil one? Pure sexism. You're both probably either bitter that Percy lost or you're Cript supporters.*

Dude, Where's My Backpack? posted: *People hate Shelly just because she's successful. They've been looking for reasons to get her expelled ever since she started at United Exceptionalism. Seriously, what kind of high schooler thinks to themselves that the best use of their time would be starting a blog against Shelly? L-O-S-E-R-S.*

\*\*\*

*The Representative* conducted another poll of how the students were feeling regarding their next potential senior class president. Fewer than one in three kids trusted anything Shelly said or did. Roughly the same amount of students described Cript as either sexist or bigoted or both. Only half of the Reformist students were enthusiastically voting for Shelly. The rest just didn't want Cript to become senior class president. Only one out of every four Traditionalist students said they were planning to vote for Cript because they liked what he had to say. The rest were voting for him because they hated McMarton. More than half of all Reformists and Traditionalists, along with all of the students who didn't fall into either of those two categories, thought both candidates were terrible options and wanted another choice.

One student wrote on her survey, "I'd gladly do additional homework if it meant neither of them became senior class president."

Another student wrote at the bottom of his survey, "If either of them becomes the next senior class president, I'm going to ask my parents if I can switch schools."

\*\*\*

Luckily for them, there was a third choice.
And a fourth choice.

# 9

While it was true that the Reformists and the Traditionalists were the dominant groups, anyone could run in the final voting round. That was part of the reason Traditionalist alumni held out hope they could find a way to sabotage Cript and get a different kid elected. But it was also how two other small factions, whom the vast majority of students had never heard of, hoped to win the election for senior class president.

The first group was the Individualists. They believed that each student at United Exceptionalism knew what was best for himself or herself and that the administration and senior class president should get out of their lives.

Jerry Hommstone was the Individualist candidate, although not many of the students really knew what an

Individualist was or where Jerry had come from. Few kids remembered actually having classes with him but the ones who did swore Jerry was one of the coolest kids to hang out with. This was mainly because his combination of aloofness and a short attention span gave the impression he was constantly high on pot.

The other choice was the Tree party. They believed the academy should switch over to solar power and be completely off the grid. They also wanted to ensure the football team was never sent to wreak havoc at another school ever again.

Nel Stipe was the Tree candidate. She wasn't as loud or passionate as Percy Wethers had been, but she did share most of his beliefs. She was also a proponent of using science and actual statistics to make decisions rather than guiding United Exceptionalism based on "how things had always been done." Nel had received detention on multiple occasions for protesting aspects of United Exceptionalism she thought needed more attention.

***

Jerry Hommstone knocked on the open door of *The Representative's* office. Chrissy Cassidy was in the room by herself, groaning each time she read another line of the garbage her freshmen and sophomores claimed to be their next articles.

"Yeah?" she said, not bothering to turn and see who was there.

"I'm running for senior class president," Jerry said, his smile audible. "I was hoping you'd be interested in doing an interview with me for the paper."

Chrissy closed her eyes for a split second. The voice was a student's but it wasn't Reginald's or Shelly's. That was all she needed to know.

"No, thanks."

"No?"

Chrissy sighed and deleted an entire paragraph that one of her freshmen had written.

"Yeah, I said no thanks."

"Well, why not?"

Chrissy's nostrils flared. She spun in her chair to see who was bothering her.

"Because the students already have their two choices. I don't want to confuse them by saying there's a third kid they've never heard of." Instead of stopping there, she added, "And who, quite frankly, has no hope of winning."

Jerry could have stated his case. He could have raised his voice so students up and down the hall heard how he was being treated.

Instead, he said, "Oh, okay," and left.

***

Only an hour later, Nel also knocked on the door leading into *The Representative's* office.

"What?" Chrissy said, disgusted by how little effort one of her sophomores had put into his article about a water fountain at United Exceptionalism that was making students sick.

"I'm running for senior class president," Nel said. "I'd like to be interviewed so the students can get a sense of what I stand for."

"No, thanks."

There was a moment of silence. Chrissy prayed that the girl at the door, whoever she was, had gone away. Her wish wasn't to come true, however.

"Why not?"

"The students voted for who they want their two choices to be. Anyone else is just a distraction."

"A distraction? I'll have you know all the same kids who got excited for Percy Wethers would love me if they knew what I stood for."

Chrissy swiveled in her chair. Rather than scowl, she laughed.

"You're forgetting one incredibly important thing."

"That is?"

"Percy couldn't even beat Shelly. The kids had a chance to pick him over her and he lost."

"The entire process was rigged."

"Ah, the famous last words of a loser."

"You're doing a disservice if you don't include a piece on me."

"Listen, it's been a hundred and fifty years since a senior class president was elected that wasn't a Reformist or a Traditionalist. I know you're used to hearing your teachers say anything is possible, but I don't like the chances of you doing something no one else has done in a century and a half."

"If you would just—"

"No."

\*\*\*

*Notes from the Underground* was happy to do interviews with both kids. Jerry Hommstone spoke about how no teenager wanted their parents telling them what to do and what not to do and said the senior class president and faculty at United Exceptionalism were just like another parent. As long as kids weren't hurting anyone else, he said, they should be allowed to do whatever they wanted.

\*\*\*

The responses posted to *Notes from the Underground's* comment section were not kind.

Shelly-4-Life posted: *Who is this Jerry Hommstone wacko and how many drugs has he done? Does anyone understand exactly how catastrophic it would be if his ideas were put into motion? What an idiot.*

True Belieber posted: *Any vote for Hommstone is a vote for Cript. You might as well say, "Hey, I want a sexist dick to be the next senior class president!" if you vote for this shmuck.*

Percy's #1 Perv posted: *This guy doesn't have a chance of winning. Sam Becksworth has a better chance of being nominated prom king than this Jerry Hommstone kid has of becoming the next senior class president (Sorry, Sam!). You might as well throw your vote away.*

\*\*\*

*Notes from the Underground* interviewed Nel Stipe next. She talked about how there was really no difference between McMarton and Cript because both were in favor of the football team beating up kids from various high schools. She also said it was disgraceful that an academy like United Exceptionalism would allow its students to drink from tainted water fountains and urged the entire campus to switch over to clean air and water solutions. Lastly, she appealed directly to all of the students who rallied around Percy Wethers and asked them to join her.

\*\*\*

Percy's #1 Perv: *My boy Percy didn't win and yet this girl's solution is to get his followers to join her so she can also not win?... smh*

Comb's Comb: *Not even Nel Stipe's mom knows who she is. Seriously, I'll be shocked if more than three people vote for this chick.*

True Belieber: *Any vote for Stipe is a vote for Cript. You're just throwing your vote away and helping Reginald.*

# 10

Every week, a new poll was released with the results of who the students at United Exceptionalism planned to vote for. The polls were coordinated through *The Representative* via the teachers in rotating classrooms. One week, the students in first period Biology, Geometry, and U.S. History were polled. The next week it would be the students in Music, P.E., and Chemistry. The results were tallied and posted later in the day on *The Representative*'s website.

When it came time for the students in Ms. Neveda's class to vote, two of them had a problem. The form started by asking what grade the student was in and if they identified as Reformist, Traditionalist, or Other. Then, in addition to asking the students who they planned to vote for between Cript or McMarton, it asked them to describe the candidates in one word. It also had a series of True/False questions.

*I consider Shelly McMarton to be an honest person. Circle one:* TRUE *or* FALSE

*I think Reginald Cript is unprepared to be senior class president. Circle one:* TRUE *or* FALSE

*I'm looking forward to voting for senior class president. Circle one:* TRUE *or* FALSE

The first student to complain was Amy Showenweiss.

"Uh, Ms. Neveda. I'm going to vote but I refuse to vote for Cript or McMarton."

"I understand, Amy. But for the purpose of this poll, who would you vote for if you had to vote for one of them?"

"I wouldn't."

"But what if you had to?"

"I wouldn't."

Ms. Neveda sighed and told Amy to leave the first question blank if she felt that strongly about it.

"Uh, Ms. Neveda?" Nel Stipe's hand was raised and her mouth was curled at the edges the same way it did when she had a question on a quiz that was too vague and could be interpreted multiple ways.

"Yes, Nel?"

"I'm running for senior class president and my name isn't on here."

"That's great!" Amy said. "I'm writing down her name then."

The History teacher took a deep breath before telling Amy that wasn't allowed. "Maybe on future papers but not this one." Then she turned to Nel and said, "The poll is just to get a sense of how the majority of the students feel about the two main choices, that's all. It's nothing personal."

"But what's the point of the poll if it doesn't show who the students would actually vote for?"

Ms. Neveda didn't answer the question. Instead, she assigned the entire class additional homework that night.

\*\*\*

*From the Editor,*

*The latest polls are out and they show a near tie between Reginald Cript and Shelly McMarton. In a sign of the times, more than half of all students expressed a lack of interest in voting for either candidate and said they had the intention of voting against one person rather than voting for someone they actually like.*

\*\*\*

Melissa and Rachel spent that evening making fun

of anyone who went on the academy's message boards to ask for more information on Hommstone or Stipe.

"We had a first round of voting for a reason," Rachel typed under the moniker *Harambe-Lives*. "And in the first round, the students picked Shelly and Reginald. So what are they bitching about now? Accept that those are the two choices. When you do, you'll see Shelly is the clear pick. You may not like her but if you don't want United Exceptionalism to go to shit, you need to vote for her."

A few kids were familiar with Hommstone and Stipe and posted messages telling everyone else to vote for one of them instead of McMarton or Cript. When this happened, Melissa and Rachel responded as quickly as possible, changing accounts to create the illusion this was a tremendously unpopular idea. Anyone who voted for the Individualists or Tree Party was throwing their votes away, they said. They insisted that a vote for either third option was nothing more than a vote that Shelly should have gotten, and any student at United Exceptionalism who voted for them deserved to have Cript as their senior class president.

\*\*\*

Anna typed the next blog post for *Notes from the Underground* while Yeri did the Calculus homework for both of them. It started:

*Our own academy's paper admits that more than half of all students aren't interested in voting for Cript or McMarton. If that's the case, why aren't they telling us more about Hommstone or Stipe?*

# 11

There were rare exceptions when students became energized in the first round of voting. Percy Wethers proved that was possible. But the reality was that most kids didn't care about who was running for senior class president until the two candidates debated each other in front of the entire academy. After that, they forgot about it again until the day they voted. Students knew that no matter who they voted for, nothing of substance would actually change.

That resigned nature, that apathetic response, was what led most of them to either vote for a major candidate whose group they identified with or else their vote was based on simple name recognition. Most years, the election for senior class president turned into a contest of which kid was disliked by more of the student body. In that regard, the race between McMarton and Cript was just more of the same.

The debate was fast approaching and students who hadn't cared so far were getting their first real glimpse of Shelly and Reginald. The students wouldn't get to see Jerry or Nel, however, because they weren't invited to the debate. Most kids assumed that not appearing at the debate proved that the Individualists and Tree Party weren't valid options. Otherwise, they would be there, right?

What the students didn't realize, though, was that two of United Exceptionalism's teachers were responsible for coordinating the debate and that one was a staunch Reformist and the other was a lifelong Traditionalist. Both wanted to ensure that only two students would have a place at the debate. To that end, they said a student had to poll at fifteen percent or higher in order to be allowed to participate in the debate.

That created a huge problem for kids like Nel and Jerry who weren't even listed on some of the polls.

\*\*\*

"Here you go," Nel said, dropping three sheets of papers on Chrissy Cassidy's desk.

"And what's this?"

"A petition. A hundred kids here want my name included on the next poll you do."

*The Representative's* editor looked over the names, flipped the first page, did the same on the second page. Her eyes darted left to right and then back again.

Nel expected a fight. She expected Chrissy to say it wasn't going to be that easy.

Instead, the editor shrugged and said, "Okay, whatever."

"You'll do it?"

"Yeah, whatever. Now if you'll leave me alone, I'm super busy."

\*\*\*

Anna and Yeri heard about Nel's success. In addition to her name being added to the next poll, Jerry Hommstone's would be as well. To counteract this development, teachers told their students as they handed out the polling forms that the only realistic options were Cript or McMarton and that any student who voted for someone else was ensuring the candidate they didn't like would win.

\*\*\*

According to the school paper, thirty-five percent

of the students polled planned to vote for Shelly. Thirty-three percent planned to vote for Cript. The article went on to mention that Shelly was peaking at just the right time. Cript, meanwhile, was supposedly in a tailspin after firing another faculty advisor. He also claimed publicly that it wasn't enough for the football team to beat up kids at other schools; if United Exceptionalism wanted to be taken seriously it would have to also beat up the families of students at other schools.

The article following that one was by the same Statistics teacher who, two weeks earlier, had said Cript's lead didn't mean anything because polling during that time of the school year was pointless. Now, however, was an important time to gauge student opinion and what Wade Copper saw clearly indicated Shelly would be the next senior class president.

***

"That's it?" Anna yelled, throwing her hands in the air. "That's it?" She looked around her room for something to break but the only things nearby were stuffed animals from her childhood, none of which would offer the satisfaction of destruction.

"I can't believe it," Yeri said. "They have no shame."

Thirty-five percent of the students said they were going to vote for Shelly and thirty-three percent said they were going to vote for Reginald. Only sixty-eight percent of the responses were mentioned. The other thirty-two percent didn't matter.

Anna turned and looked at Yeri. In her eyes he saw the real world shattering her hopes.

"Is it too late to transfer to another academy?" she asked.

He put his arms around her.

# 12

"You've got to get out there and be seen," Mr. Podulski said.

Shelly's faculty advisor had a stack of notes next to him, and although Shelly was never allowed to see them, she got the feeling they were filled with the comments of various Reformist alumni, each telling Mr. Podulski what they wanted Shelly to say and do. Rumor had it that more and more Traditionalist alumni were also reaching out to see how they could support Shelly and to find out what she would do for them in return when she was elected.

"You told me to stay out of sight," she said with her characteristic hint of a sneer.

"I told you to minimize how much the students see and hear you because it's your best way of winning." He said this to her as if she wouldn't understand just how insulting it was. He added, "But you've taken it further than you should have. What we want is for you not to commit on any issue affecting the academy. But what you're doing is coming off as being completely separate from the students who are going to vote. You don't attend your classes. You don't do interviews with *The Representative*. You aren't participating in any after-school activities. Don't go overboard, just start going to classes and saying hi to kids in the hallway."

\*\*\*

Running for senior class president wasn't as easy as it sounded. Each student still had to study for classes, keep their room clean, and grapple with puberty. Just because Shelly hadn't been attending classes didn't mean she was skipping all of her quizzes and homework. The teachers were allowing her to study in the quiet of the academy library where she wouldn't be bothered.

Following Mr. Podulski's edict, Shelly was in a room full of her peers for her English class when her head began to hurt. Her temples ached. It wasn't a throbbing. Instead, it was like a hand squeezing her entire skull. She put her head down on her desk and closed her eyes.

\*\*\*

"How's it going?" Shelly said to Jenny West as she walked to her next class.

Her throat itched and she coughed.

"Nice sweater!" she said to Destiny Armstead as they both arrived to their Ancient History class.

The tickle in her throat taunted her, forced her to cough again. As soon as she did, her esophagus felt raw, as if she'd been coughing for hours already.

To make matters worse, the headache was still making it difficult for her to keep her eyes open. Every muscle felt fatigued, as if she had gym class six times a day.

She raised her hand.

"Yes, Shelly?" Ms. Vernon said.

"I've got a headache. Can I go to the nurse?"

"Sure."

Shelly packed her book and notes into her backpack. Her legs were so sore and tired that she didn't feel like walking, wished someone would carry her to the nurse. On her way out of the room, she stumbled, bumped her shoulder against the doorway, then paused and braced herself before continuing.

\*\*\*

Rumors spread from classroom to classroom the way they did when a popular couple broke up or two boys

214

were going to fight in the parking lot after school. Shelly had barely been seen for weeks and now that she was back she was stumbling, complaining of headaches, and had a raspy voice.

It was obvious what was happening. She was dying.

***

Rachel and Melissa were standing at Rachel's locker. From the outside it looked like any other locker. But on the inside was a paper filled with account names and passwords for all of the mischief they caused.

"She's so self-centered," Melissa said of Shelly. "She'd go through this entire election and become senior class president just to die two days later and waste everyone's time. To her, everything is Shelly, Shelly, Shelly."

Rachel looked around to make sure no one but her friend was close enough to hear, then whispered. "My dad better still give me that car he owes me if she dies, you know?"

***

Someone associated with Shelly's campaign posted a message to her Facebook page. Shelly was fine. She was just tired from cramming for a quiz and from not sleeping well the night before. She was resting comfortably in the nurse's office.

***

Two hours later, the door to the nurse's office opened and a smiling and exuberant Shelly appeared.

"How ya doin'?" she said to a freshman who was working off her detention by filing papers in the academy's administrative offices.

The girl's face was pure confusion—only two hours earlier Shelly had told the girl to get the hell out of the way. Shelly laughed and went across the reception room to where a senior was reloading a printer with paper. She smiled and said hello to him as well, then left.

\*\*\*

Minutes later, another message was posted to Shelly's Facebook page. This one said Shelly had been treated by the nurse and was feeling excellent once again. In fact, she had a doctor's note that said she had been diagnosed with mononucleosis two days earlier and had been feeling the side effects from her medication.

\*\*\*

Anna read that post and didn't know whether to laugh or cry.

"Mono? Now they're saying she has mono? Two hours ago they said she was just tired? Do they even realize how contagious mono is, and yet she's walking around school like it doesn't matter how many other people get infected?"

\*\*\*

*From the Editor,*

*We at The Representative have covered hundreds of students who ran for senior class president but we've never covered someone with the tenacity of Shelly McMarton, who is so determined to lead United Exceptionalism into the future that she fought through a recent illness without missing any school. Anyone thinking of voting for Jerry Hommstone or Nel Stipe should remember the toughness Shelly showed this week because it's the same ferocity she'll show when she's leading this academy.*

# 13

"You know," Cript said, standing at a cafeteria table full of tenth grade boys, each of whom was already laughing in expectation of what he was going to say next, "they call mono 'the kissing disease.' Who in their right mind would kiss Shelly?"

A group of girls was sitting at the next table over. They all thought Cript was sleazy and sexist and none of them would ever vote for him, but they laughed as well because no one liked Shelly.

Having performed long enough at one table, Cript made his way toward them. Each girl stopped smiling. None of them said hello, and most of them envisioned their boyfriends punching Cript in the face.

"You know what really gets me?" Cript asked them. "First Shelly said she had a headache and then she was just tired and then she had already been diagnosed with mono two days earlier. It just shows you can't trust a single thing she says."

Although they hadn't wanted to, the girls found themselves nodding in agreement.

"Reminds me of a girl I dated one time," Cript added. "Mind you, she wasn't a dog like Shelly—although she also wasn't as attractive as any of you ladies."

He smiled and winked when he said things like that. In his mind, each girl was playing hard to get and secretly adored him. He had no idea that the goose bumps on their arms were the same kind they got when watching horror movies.

At the next table, Reginald said to a group of senior boys, "McMarton's just weak. It's pathetic, really. I attend school each day too. You don't see me crying about it. She just can't stand up to the pressure. Not me, though. I could run a marathon right now."

***

Cript said the same kinds of things over the course of the next week. While he still mocked McMarton, he kept his insults on a less derogatory level than usual. He didn't insinuate that someone might want to kill her. He didn't alienate himself from any new segment of United Exceptionalism's student body.

By simply not being as mean or juvenile as he normally was, he retook the lead in the next round of student polling.

***

Wade Copper, the Statistics teacher, immediately posted an article on *The Representative* that said the polls were flawed and could be ignored.

***

Yeri read the results of the latest poll to Anna.

"In one classroom, of the twenty-seven students polled, fourteen said they'd vote for Cript and thirteen said they'd vote for Shelly."

Anna closed her eyes and sighed. She knew what had happened; the teacher, whoever it had been, had only given the students two options.

Yeri said, "In another classroom, of the twenty-six students polled, nine said they'd vote for Cript and eight said they'd vote for McMarton."

Anna pressed her fingers into her eyes until a burst of colors appeared behind her eyelids.

"That leaves nine kids that they won't say who they'd vote for."

"Yes, it does."

***

While the important alumni who usually supported Traditionalist candidates were still remaining silent, Cript did pick up one endorsement.

"I'm going to vote for Reginald," Chet Booth said.

The reporter from *The Representative* could barely stifle her yawn.

"He ridiculed you in front of the entire school. He made fun of your little sister and your imaginary girlfriend and—"

"I have a girlfriend!"

"Okay, sure. Either way, you said you'd never support him."

Chet nodded and looked out the window of the empty classroom he had commandeered for the interview.

"Yeah, but it's the best thing for United Exceptionalism, so I have to do it."

The girl clicked her pen shut and rolled her eyes.

"Okay, whatever." She stood up. "Did you have anything else earth-shattering you wanted to say?"

Chet's lips disappeared behind a wall of fat. He looked down at the floor.

"No," he mumbled.

# 14

McMarton and Cript were already the two least popular candidates running for senior class president in the history of United Exceptionalism. One poll showed that two percent of all students were actually considering transferring schools. Another poll showed that if any other student were the Reformist candidate instead of Shelly, he or she would easily beat Cript. Another showed that if any other Traditionalist candidate were to run against Shelly, they too would easily win. Three quarters of all students wanted a third or fourth option.

\*\*\*

Everywhere Anna and Yeri went, they saw students in every grade who were disgusted at having to choose between two awful choices.

Yeri remembered that his chemistry partner was opposed to the football team ever going off like hired goons again. The flame at the Bunsen burner in front of them glowed blue.

"Well, that's what Jerry Hommstone believes, too," he told the kid. "Shelly and Reginald both want the football team to settle every problem we have. You could vote for Jerry and you'd be supporting someone who believes in the same thing as you."

The kid gave a disinterested snort and sprinkled white powder on the flame, which flashed a sparkling blue.

"He's not gonna win," the boy said. "I'd be throwing my vote away."

"So you're gonna end up voting for McMarton or Cript?"

The boy shrugged. "I'll probably just skip school that day."

\*\*\*

Anna was in her Art class, using watercolors to paint a vase of flowers. Next to her, a junior jabbed a brush at her canvas, creating an impressionist tree.

"You liked Percy Wethers, didn't you?" Anna said to the girl.

"Yeah, why?"

"Nel Stipe believes in most of the same stuff Percy believed in. You could vote for her and support someone you actually like instead of someone you don't."

The girl rubbed her brush into a brown pod of paint, then smacked in against the canvas. A tree trunk had just been created.

"But she's not gonna win," the young Van Gogh said. "If I vote for her and Cript ends up winning, I'll be partly responsible."

\*\*\*

After their last class, Anna and Yeri searched the halls for Percy Wethers.

"He must have left already," Yeri said.

Anna pointed over his shoulder at a tall boy lumbering with a backpack slung over one shoulder.

"Percy," Anna called down the hallway and waved to him.

Wethers looked around, saw them, and smiled.

"How's it going?" Percy said after making his way toward them, an untroubled smile on his face.

"Good," Yeri said. "We're going to do an article tonight and we wanted to ask you some questions."

"Fire away."

Anna pulled out a pad of paper.

"What's your reasoning for voting for Nel Stipe when everyone says it's either throwing a vote away or else it's a vote for Cript?"

Percy's forehead crinkled into a ball of creases.

"Well, uh, I'm not voting for Nel. I'm sure she's nice and all, but I'm voting for Shelly."

The air left Anna's lungs. Yeri stared at Percy as if waiting for an alien to burst from his stomach. Percy bobbed his head as he looked back and forth between the two reporters.

"But Nel stands for most of the same stuff you did," Anna said.

"Yeah."

She shook her head and added, "And you said Shelly was everything the academy should move away from."

"Yeah..."

"So why, then?"

"Look," Percy said, his tone becoming slightly annoyed. "We have to do everything we can to make sure Cript isn't elected."

"By voting for a girl you yourself pointed out as having a terrible record of supporting ideas that set the academy back? Even though there's another candidate who stands for almost exactly what you stood for?"

"Listen, we have to defeat Cript. We can't be idealistic. The only two viable choices are Cript or McMarton so there's no choice at all; we have to elect McMarton."

"But nobody thought you had a chance," she said. "You used to stand up in the gymnasium and tell the kids how nobody gave you a shot and you almost won. Now you're saying someone else can't do the same thing?"

Yeri put a hand on her shoulder. It was only then that she realized she had raised her voice to the point that she was almost yelling.

Percy sighed. "What else can I say? We need to

defeat Cript and I think McMarton is the best person to do that."

Wethers smiled at them, hoping they might be able to return the gesture. When neither of them did, his shoulders dropped and he turned and began walking away.

\*\*\*

After school that evening, Anna went over to Yeri's house and the two of them took turns typing on his computer. They did this for an hour without pause. For the next two hours after that, they edited each other's writing, moved paragraphs around, and asked each other questions.

Yeri's mom appeared at his bedroom door.

"Wouldn't you kids like some dinner?"

Without looking away from the screen, he replied, "No thanks, Mom. Busy."

\*\*\*

The piece they posted to *Notes from the Underground* was the longest they'd written. In it, they dispelled common myths that stated everyone had to vote for either McMarton or Cript and proved their case that Hommstone's and Stipe's ideas were more in line with what the average student actually believed, regardless of whether they considered themselves Reformist or Traditionalist.

*A vote for Stipe is not a vote for Cript. It's simply a vote for Stipe. It's a vote that says students believe our football team shouldn't be involved in more violence. It's a vote for ensuring the water at our drinking fountains is safe.*

*A vote for Hommstone isn't a vote for Shelly. It's just a vote for Hommstone. It's a vote for everyone who's tired of the academy telling students what they can and can't do.*

*These are things the majority of students want. Meanwhile, McMarton and Cript both support a range of ideas that most students at United Exceptionalism don't agree with. So, who would you rather have as your next senior class president?*

They railed against the idea that only a candidate with the Traditionalist T next to their name or the Reformist R could possibly become senior class president.

*Everywhere you go, teachers tell you that only two viable options exist. The school paper tells you that only McMarton or Cript can become the next senior class president for no better reason than they're the Reformist and Traditionalist candidates. As if some magic wand has been waved and no other options, even though they exist, could possibly be worthy. The truth is, it would be incredibly easy for either Hommstone or Stipe to win. All the students would have to do is check a box with their name next to it instead of a box with McMarton's or Cript's name next to it.*

*Talk about easy! Consider the things students at United Exceptionalism have managed to do over the years. Two have gone on to win Pulitzers. Dozens have gone on to become state and national politicians. One created a cure for a disease. Another created a high efficiency solar panel. Compared to those things, simply checking off a different box is the easiest thing we can do.*

They explained how other academies had more than two options and how those institutions seemed to be getting along just fine.

*There are many private schools with academic success equal to or greater than United Exceptionalism's. What do they have in common? They don't limit themselves to only two options for senior class president. Some have four or five options. These schools will tell you that the more choices students have, the better leadership they're able to find. And still, United Exceptionalism does everything it can to insist there are only two choices, even going so far as to prevent a third or fourth option from attending the upcoming debate.*

## The Faulty Process of Electing a Senior Class President

*In some schools, they even have tiered voting for senior class president, where students rank each option. That way, students are assured of voting for someone they like instead of getting scared into voting against someone they don't like. Yet everywhere you go at United Exceptionalism, you're told it's not realistic. Maybe we should start asking why teachers and alumni are so set on keeping things the way they are.*

When they were done, they clicked PUBLISH and waited for the responses.

\*\*\*

Unfortunately for them, Rachel and Melissa were bored and looking for something to do. Rachel typed the first response, a message that said Anna still watched cartoons and that anything she said should be ignored. Melissa typed a message saying Yeri sounded like someone Homeland Security might want to speak with and that he obviously wanted to ruin United Exceptionalism's traditions. Both took turns saying there was no way students would all vote for some pot smoker who was obviously tired of his parents telling him what to do or for some hippie who wanted peace, love, and tranquility. They also took turns saying that whether you hated them or not, Cript and McMarton were the only two real choices.

# 15

It seemed an impossible feat for either McMarton or Cript to become even more unpopular than they already were but, to the dismay of the students at United Exceptionalism, not just one of them but both managed to do just that. Shockingly, it was for the same reason: their charities were up to no good.

As Mr. Mailer, one of the janitors at the academy said, "Just when you think it can't get any worse for this damn place, we get screwed even harder. Pardon my French."

\*\*\*

In theory, McMarton's charity was designed to collect money and resources from the wealthy alumni of United Exceptionalism and distribute it throughout the community. Doctors went to some of the poor areas on the other side of town and gave free checkups. Medicine was given to senior citizens who couldn't afford it.

The success of her charity and how it brought people together was one of the reasons Shelly was touted as the best choice for senior class president.

But then, as with everything she was involved with, a huge and avoidable problem arose.

\*\*\*

It turned out that much of the charity was a pay-for-play scheme. The alumni who contributed money, resources, or time found themselves on the receiving end of promises from Shelly. When she became senior class president, a wealthy donor who owned a plumbing company would win the new plumbing contract for the academy. Another alumnus, the owner of an electrical company, would win the next electrical contract. The same thing went with the food vendors, roofers, lawn maintenance, security companies, even the financial investment and planning services.

While people might have assumed this was happening, it only became verified because the entire school got to see Shelly's private Facebook messages. She insisted hackers from another school must have broken into her account. Her faculty advisor said it was obvious that someone from Sovereign Union, a private school that had been rivals with United Exceptionalism decades earlier, must have been behind it. In reality, she had checked her account from the academy's library and simply forgotten to sign out. The next kid at the computer saw her messages on the screen, realized how important they were, and forwarded them to dozens of other students, who in turn made sure the rest of United Exceptionalism saw them.

It wasn't pretty. While the charity did do some good, it also showed Shelly's clear intention to reward the donors and alumni once she became senior class president.

Or did it? Not according to Shelly's mother, who posted a message saying that only *a lot* of the donors were promised favors in return, not *all* of them.

Mr. Podulski chimed in that just because the messages were from Shelly's Facebook page didn't mean she had written them.

*The Representative* took the stance that Shelly's charity should be shut down if she became senior class president because then, and only then, would it cause potential conflicts of interest.

*Notes from the Underground* posted an article that provided the dictionary definition of corruption and then posted direct quotes from Shelly's Facebook messages in which she promised the alumni contracts if they gave her money.

*** 

Only a couple hours after the charity corruption was discovered, more faculty and alumni began to blame the Sovereign Union Private School. Two decades earlier, the Sovereign Union and United Exceptionalism football teams had been rivals. Now, they wanted to renew the rivalry!

It sounded absurd and there was no proof to back up the claim, but that didn't stop *The Representative* from running with the story. Melissa and Rachel did their part by saying that if Sovereign Union wanted Cript to win—which they obviously did because they had leaked Shelly's messages—it was all the more reason to vote for McMarton. By the end of the day, half the academy was pretty sure Sovereign Union was trying to influence United Exceptionalism's election for senior class president.

***

Cript claimed that he could do anything Shelly did even better than she could. When it came to problems with his charity, that was certainly true.

# 16

Reginald's charity wasn't exchanging donations for favors; it was a place for people to throw away their money. Set up by Reginald's father and run mostly by one of his father's employees, the charity was supposed to give to a variety of worthwhile causes. One of the things Cript loved bragging about the most was how much money they donated, mainly because it was a way of earning a free pass to say and do outrageous things. When he suggested someone might want to kill a fellow classmate, he followed it up by reminding everyone he also donated a lot of money. If he promised to isolate all of the female students who wore jeans, he also noted the thousands of his own dollars he had donated to good causes. His charity gave students an excuse to overlook his sexism and bigotry and instead call him a philanthropist.

As with all things Cript, however, the wheels eventually fell off.

***

It turned out Cript's charity wasn't donating nearly as much as it said it was. Instead of hundreds of thousands of dollars, it had donated less than two hundred bucks. And, it turned out, none of the money being donated was actually Cript's; it was all from alumni who thought they were writing matching donations. Most of the money people had donated to the charity was used to buy Reginald a new Nintendo, big screen television, sports car, and even a life-size painting of himself as Tom Cruise's character in *Mission: Impossible*, Cript's favorite movie.

Unlike Shelly's corruption coming to light because

of the internet, Cript's unraveled entirely because of his own doing.

He had Romana Gunderson at his house and wanted to impress her enough to let him put his hand under her sweater. His father's big house hadn't done the trick. Neither had the art or the expensive furniture or the portrait that some German guy had done of him. Seeing that material possessions wouldn't tame Gunderson and her great mountains, he decided to go for bravado.

"You know my charity?" he whispered as they stood by his refrigerator and he saw her looking at her watch. "It's for suckers. I don't contribute anything. It's all my dad's friends. And we use it to buy awesome stuff."

His imagined best-case scenario was that she would view him as a young troublemaker. Girls loved bad boys. Another possibility was that she would want to join in something naughty, like all the wives in the gangster movies he watched.

Instead, her eyes widened and she said, "That's awful. You should be ashamed of yourself."

"Ah, come on. Don't be such a twat."

He said it with his winning smile but it had been too much. Not only had she left without letting him feel her up, she had gone straight to her dad, who had gone to the local authorities to discuss opening a formal investigation.

\*\*\*

To make matters worse, it turned out that Cript was paying nothing in tuition. Other parents were paying tens of thousands of dollars to send their children to United Exceptionalism. Even though Cript's father was richer than anyone else, his son was somehow getting a free ride.

This came to light when Chrissy Cassidy got to the office of *The Representative* and found a brown envelope on her desk. When she opened it and pulled out the paper-clipped pages, she saw they were Reginald's admission report. She didn't wait two seconds before she scanned it and published it to the school newspaper's website.

The title of the article was: ANOTHER DISASTER FOR REGINALD: PAYS ZERO WHILE YOUR PARENTS SPEND THEIR HARD-EARNED MONEY!

\*\*\*

No one questioned where the copy of Cript's paperwork had come from even though there was only one way it could have gotten from the academy's own filing cabinets to the desk of *The Representative's* editor. No one blamed the Sovereign Union Private School. It wasn't important how the information was leaked, only that it further illustrated how every part of Reginald's life was revolved around bettering himself rather than caring about what happened to the academy.

\*\*\*

@TheRealCript, 11:10 pm – Nobody knows how to use admission loopholes better than me. Just shows I'm the only person who can fix the broken system.

\*\*\*

By the end of the week, Shelly once again had a slight lead in the polls. Both she and Cript had experienced embarrassing divulgements at United Exceptionalism and yet it had helped her and hurt him.

The only reason Anna and Yeri could think of for the boost was that the students already expected McMarton to be dishonest. They had suspected she was running for senior class president in order to help herself instead of the academy. The disclosures only confirmed what many had already assumed.

On the other hand, Cript had been viewed as immature, a chauvinist, and a bully, but the majority of the kids at United Exceptionalism, even the ones who hated him, had thought of him as genuine to a fault. Now they saw that not only was he an egomaniac and skirt-chaser, he was also a con man. A con boy.

# 17

With only a week before the debate, the next poll came out. *The Representative* provided the results.

*Of the twenty-eight students in Mr. Iola's class, fifteen said they would vote for Shelly McMarton. Thirteen said they would vote for Reginald Cript. In Ms. Hampen-Shiar's class, where twenty-seven students were polled, ten said they would vote for McMarton and nine said they would vote for Cript.*

\*\*\*

Nel found Jerry Hommstone standing at his open locker. He looked as though he had forgotten something important but couldn't remember what it was and hoped time would be his friend and help him remember.

"Did you see the latest polls?" Nel asked.

Jerry blinked back into the here and now. "Oh, hi, Nel."

"In Mr. Iola's class, students didn't have the option of saying if they'd vote for anyone other than Shelly or Reginald. In Ms. Hampen-Shiar's class, they did, but the school paper won't let the kids know how many students are interested in voting for us."

"Yeah."

Nel waited there for a moment. When she realized that was all Jerry intended to say, she asked what he was going to do about it.

"Things'll work out, Nel. Just relax."

She closed her eyes and took a deep breath. When she reopened them, she said they were running out of time and that she was going to both of the teachers who organized the debate to let them know she and Jerry should be a part of it.

"You should join me."

"Nah, I'll pass, Nel. They'll do the right thing."

***

Nel knew, though, that the two teachers—one a Reformist and one a Traditionalist—had no reason to let Jerry or herself in.

She went to Mr. Fornia's classroom first. He was sitting at his desk, shaking his head while reading a student's quiz answer.

"Mr. Fornia."

"Nel."

She laid a couple of sheets of paper on his desk. "These are the names of students who would like me included in the debate."

"I'm sorry. You have to have at least fifteen percent of the students saying they might vote for you."

"How am I supposed to do that when half the polls only allow the kids to pick between McMarton and Cript?"

He nodded as if this was an ancient riddle no one had ever been able to solve.

"That's a really good question. I wish I could help,

but rules are rules."

"But you helped make the rules."

He nodded again.

***

She went to Ms. Otah's classroom next. The History teacher was standing at a window, looking out at the birds flying back and forth among the branches of a nearby tree.

"Ms. Otah," Nel said, handing her a photocopy of the list of students who didn't want Cript or McMarton to be the only debate participants. "Seventy-five percent of students at United Exceptionalism want to have a third or fourth choice for senior class president. Please let Jerry and I participate in the debate so everyone can hear our stance on the issues."

"Oh, that." M. Otah sighed and turned away from the birds. "I wish I could help but students have to have a realistic chance of winning in order to be allowed to participate in the debate."

"Seventy-five percent of kids want another option. And all they have to do is put a checkmark next to a different box. Sounds realistic to me."

"Because you're young," Ms. Otah said, still smiling. "Trust me, Nel. I've seen many kids who wanted to be a third option and they never win. Do you want my advice?" She offered it without waiting for a response. "Focus on your class work. Hang out with your friends. Enjoy your time in high school. It'll be over before you know it. But stop wasting time on this idea of becoming senior class president because you'll only be disappointed in the end."

The smile that had originally welcomed Nel was now making her enraged with how dismissive it was. There were a lot of things she wanted to say but knew none of them would make a difference. She turned and began toward the door.

"Don't forget your papers," Ms. Otah said.

"You keep them. The students would want to know their voices were heard."

\*\*\*

*From the Editor,*

*The time and location for the debate between Shelly McMarton and Reginald Cript has been set. All students will be excused from class to attend. There was a last ditch attempt by two other candidates to participate in the debate but they didn't come close to meeting the fifteen percent requirement.*

\*\*\*

That night, Anna and Yeri posted their next entry to *Notes from the Underground*. It started:

*Fewer than one in three Reformist students are excited to vote for Shelly McMarton. Two out of every three Traditionalist students say they're disgusted by the things Reginald Cript says. And yet these two students are pushed on us as the only two options for senior class president. The alumni and faculty would have you believe it's impossible for anyone else to win but it's quite easy. They would tell you that the academy wouldn't function under leadership other than from Reformists or Traditionalists. First, that's not true. Second, if it were true, it's an indictment of the system and not of Jerry Hommstone or Nel Stipe.*

*Imagine a scenario in which the two main choices for senior class president were Hitler and Satan. If that were the case, half the faculty would try to convince you that Hitler wasn't nearly as bad as Satan because he doesn't rule over the pits of hell. The other half of the faculty would try to convince you that Satan wasn't as bad as Hitler because he didn't kill millions of Jews, gypsies, and homosexuals. Never once would the two sides allow the students at this academy to consider the idea that someone else might actually be*

235

*a better choice. In fact, they would do everything in their power to keep you divided between two terrible options that they insist are the only two realistic choices.*

# 18

As the students filed into the gym for the debate, most were looking forward to the spectacle and the guaranteed laughs it would offer more than any kind of serious discussion on the future of United Exceptionalism. The teachers were able to easily identify the few students who actually cared about which policies the academy adopted because they weren't smiling. Some looked like they wanted to cry.

\*\*\*

"I can't wait for Reginald to tear into her. It's going to be ninety minutes of him making fun of her weight, her looks, the ex-boyfriend who cheated on her, and all the lies she's constantly telling. She's going to have to sit there and be ridiculed in front of the entire school and there's nothing she's going to be able to do about it."

\*\*\*

"Do you realize just how dumb Cript is? Shelly's going to mention specific ideas she has for United Exceptionalism and he's going to stand there with a stupid look on his face, and when he does say something, he's going to misuse the same words he always uses incorrectly. I hope she calls him out on all of his sexism in front of everyone."

***

Nel watched from the edge of the gymnasium. Many students were still filing into the rows of bleachers. On the far side of the gym, Shelly and Reginald began to walk across the floor, toward the pair of lecterns and microphones. Nel started toward them as well.

A hand caught her elbow before she could take two steps.

"Where do you think you're going?"

It was Vice Principal McHendricks and he looked none too pleased at her obvious attempt to crash the party.

"I need to go out there," she said, her gaze riveted on the podium.

"What you need to do," he said, his throat scratchy, on the verge of a coughing fit, "is to report to the library for quiet time. If you're seen back here, you'll have to explain yourself to the Director of Student Affairs."

"But—"

"Do I make myself clear?"

Nel's eyes lowered. All around her, students began to clap for the two main candidates.

"Yeah," she said, her response inaudible over the clamor of the packed room.

***

Of the few students who noticed the vice principal talking to Nel, only Anna and Yeri actually knew who Nel was. The rest just figured she hadn't turned in a report that was due or hadn't completed her homework and thus wasn't allowed to attend the debate.

Anna leaned toward her boyfriend and said, "She's

237

being taken away like she's the class clown."

Yeri shook his head, the air fleeing his lungs. "These aren't the candidates we want, but they're the candidates we deserve."

\*\*\*

No one saw or heard from Jerry Hommstone during the debate. He didn't try to force his way onto the stage the way Nel had. Rumor was he was smoking pot with a couple other kids out behind the track and field area.

\*\*\*

As with all spectacles that promised to be miraculous and disturbing, the debate left the majority of students and faculty unsatisfied. Even after all the vicious attacks the two sides had leveled at each other the entire school year, McMarton and Cript shook hands and smiled as if they were old buddies. Everyone in attendance understood then that they were seeing nothing more than live-action reality television playing out in front of them.

Cript pointed out a few things Shelly was unpopular for, but for the most part spoke about his father's wealth and about how good he was at everything. Shelly spent one minute saying how unqualified Cript was to be senior class president, but most of the time she talked in generalities about how the world was changing and United Exceptionalism had evolve with it.

The few times Shelly was called out for her lies she denied them even though there was proof of what she had said. No one—not Cript and not a member of the faculty—corrected her. When all of Cript's lies were pointed out, he denied the accusations even though there was video and audio of him saying everything he was denying. Again, no one forced him to be accountable for what he had said and done.

Neither McMarton nor Cript mentioned the water fountain that was toxic and making kids sick.

Neither of them mentioned how deeply in debt the academy was or the troubles the football team was causing.

Neither of them said much, really, of anything.

When it was over, the students sighed and filed out of the gymnasium so they wouldn't be late for their next class.

***

Of the students who were polled on their way out of the gymnasium, forty-two percent said they didn't believe their vote mattered. A third said they might skip school the day of the voting.

When asked if they would consider voting for someone other than McMarton or Cript, a common response was, "I guess not. If they weren't at the debate they must not have a chance of winning."

# 19

"What am I watching?" Anna said, squinting at the Youtube video playing on her smart phone.

It showed a hazy white blur that seemed to be moving. The video came into focus and the object was apparently a door. Yeri looked at the user name of the person who had posted it. It was CONCERNED STUDENT.

"I still don't get what this is supposed to be show—"

She stopped when she heard a familiar voice amidst the din in the background. It was Reginald Cript. The image went in and out of focus, but she eventually realized whoever recorded it had been at one of Cript's parties.

"When you're as popular and rich as I am, you can get away with anything," Reginald said from the other side of the door. "I just love kissing girls. I don't even care if they want me to kiss them, I just go up to them and put my tongue in their mouth. If they don't like it, that's their problem."

He paused for a moment while the other boys in the room laughed at what he was saying.

"You can do anything when you're Reginald Cript. You know what one of my favorite moves is? I just grab their butthole."

More laughing.

"Not their ass, mind you. Their butthole. That's my move. And I get away with it."

More laughing.

The video ended.

Even though the video was over, Anna stared at

the screen, shell shocked by what she had just heard. Yeri shook his head and groaned.

"I have a feeling I know what everyone at school will be talking about tomorrow," he said.

***

At nearly the same time Anna and Yeri listened to the audio of Cript at one of his parties, and as the same video spread like wildfire across the rest of the academy, another revelation came out.

More leaked emails from United Exceptionalism's faculty and administration were released. Many were from Mr. Podulski's account and showed the type of guidance he gave to the rest of the staff on how to address certain topics concerning Shelly McMarton. In one, he acknowledged that what Shelly told the students was diametrically opposed to what she was telling alumni behind closed doors. He also told some of the teachers what to say to *The Representative* and how the school newspaper should cover each topic. Everything that was reported about Shelly should paint her as the voice of the students and the reliable, experienced option, while everything about Reginald should paint him as a loose cannon and a pig.

Worst of all were the emails from Shelly herself. In one, she mocked people who believed in God. In another, she mocked people who didn't believe in God. In one she referred to Reformists as losers and in another she referred to Traditionalists as loons.

***

"So basically what the emails prove," Yeri said, all of the energy in his body escaping him, "is that everything we've suspected is true. Shelly can't be trusted. *The Representative* is just a tool. And everyone's in on it."

241

Anna's shoulders slumped. Her eyelids felt heavy and part of her wished she didn't care about this revelation or who the next senior class president would be.

"Pretty much," she said.

\*\*\*

*The Representative* had a field day with the Cript video. They posted the link for any student who hadn't already seen it. They interviewed the Sex Education teacher, who said Cript's language and behavior suggested deep-rooted issues with women. They interviewed some of his ex-girlfriends under the condition their names wouldn't be printed. Each girl confirmed that Cript had been aggressive with them and had constantly said and done lewd things.

\*\*\*

In addition to the headlines about Cript and the dozen different "Just grab their buttholes" stories they ran, *The Representative* also posted this message about Shelly:

*Another batch of faculty emails has been released. We cannot confirm if they are actual emails or just an attempt by the Sovereign Union Private School to further influence this election. Shelly was not directly implicated in any wrongdoing by anything in the emails.*

\*\*\*

There wasn't much else for Anna and Yeri to add on top of everything that was said about Cript. Their only contribution was going back and analyzing all the things Reginald had stated about girls who wore jeans, about wanting to humiliate them by building barriers around them in class, and then mentioning that it should have been obvious all along the type of kid he was.

After all the hateful and sexist things Reginald had said that had earned laughs and scorn, it was a comment about grabbing girls' buttholes that finally cast a cloud over him. It wasn't being openly sexist or wanting to isolate a segment of the student body. It wasn't saying that the football team should not only terrorize kids at other schools but also their unsuspecting family members. It was bragging about molesting girls.

*\*\**

Anna and Yeri got to school early the next day to talk to Shelly's faculty advisor.

"Ah, the junior reporters," the Economics teacher said when he heard a knock at his door and looked up to see them.

It was true that they were in eleventh grade, but Anna didn't think Mr. Podulski was referring to that. She suspected he was instead implying that she and Yeri were somehow lesser journalists than the kids who wrote for the official school paper.

"We'd like to ask you a couple questions," Yeri said.

"I bet you would."

But instead of telling them he was too busy, Podulski motioned for them to come in and take a seat.

"There were more leaked emails," Anna said. "Concerning the Reformist efforts to get Shelly elected."

Mr. Podulski shook his head and sighed. "Isn't it disgusting that someone is trying to influence the election by posting that stuff?"

"Don't you think the students have a right to know if Shelly is telling them one thing and then privately telling the alumni something else?"

"Really, that's beside the point. All these emails do is help Cript get elected."

Anna scanned the questions they had thought to ask and then picked one of the more important ones in case Mr. Podulski dismissed them again.

"So you're confirming the emails were yours?"

The Economics teacher shrugged. "I don't know. I don't have the time to see if they were mine or just something that was made up."

"But what's more important than checking to see if they are real?"

Mr. Podulski narrowed his eyes. "Other than ensuring Reginald Cript isn't elected? Other than that, I suppose it's a valid topic. But I really am too busy to check all of my emails against the ones that were released." He looked down at his watch then said, "Speaking of being busy."

Anna and Yeri knew what was coming next and were already standing to leave his classroom.

*** 

After school that day, the couple went to Anna's house to write another post for *Notes from the Underground*. Each time they tried to come up with a story about the latest McMarton email leaks, they found there was nothing to write about. Everyone already knew McMarton was dishonest; her entire charity was proof of that. There was nothing else to add to what they had already covered.

Instead, they found themselves talking about Cript and "Just grab them by the butthole."

"We already posted about that too," Yeri said.

Ten minutes later, they still had nothing written about Mr. Podulski's emails or anything else.

"What else can we write about?" she asked.

The only thing she kept thinking about was that any other Reformist candidate would easily defeat Cript and the academy wouldn't have to worry about being subjected to his whims. And as soon as that thought entered her mind, the complimentary idea struck back—any other Traditionalist candidate would easily defeat McMarton and the academy wouldn't have to worry about a senior class president who was entirely corrupt.

Yeri saw her caught in the same loop of angst that had come over nearly the entire student body and said, "Maybe we've written everything there is to write."

She put her head on his shoulder and closed her eyes. "And it didn't make any difference at all, did it? No one cares."

He reached over and took hold of her hand. Deep down, they both knew what the answer was, but Yeri went ahead and said it anyway.

"No matter what we wrote, it was going to be McMarton and Cript and one of them was going to be our senior class president next year."

Anna opened her eyes again. They were red and irritated and Yeri saw she was on the verge of tears.

"There are a lot of other good schools."

He nodded and said there were.

"We could transfer."

\*\*\*

The students of United Exceptionalism were left to decide between a girl they didn't like or trust, who made fun of the very people she hoped would vote for her, but who didn't molest people, and a boy they didn't like, didn't want to be associated with, and who laughed about groping girls.

In that sad decision lay the future of United Exceptionalism.

# 20

Two days before the election, Cript's support seemed to be at an all time low. Everywhere he went, United Exceptionalism's students yelled variations of "Grab them by the butthole."

Half of the kids detested Reginald and sneered as they said it. "Don't try to grab my butthole, you sicko."

The other half laughed and shook their fist in the air in solidarity. "We're gonna make this academy great again, one butthole at a time, right?"

\*\*\*

Backed into a corner, the focus of relentless mockery, Cript knew of only one course to take.

"The entire election is rigged," he told everyone who would listen. "The entire process is a sham. The faculty wants Shelly to win. The alumni want her to win. I never had a chance!"

As with everything else Reginald said, those who were disgusted by him saw a loser who didn't know how to deal with his own shortcomings while all of his supporters believed the election for senior class president would be a travesty of the academy's honor code.

\*\*\*

*We at The Representative have previously seen candidates for senior class president who didn't like the outcome of the election. We have also seen students who made some questionable comments while they sought to become our next student leader. But we have never seen or heard something so dangerous as what Reginald Cript said earlier today in declaring that the election for senior class president might be rigged. That kind of rhetoric begs for unrest and for his supporters to doubt the validity of the election even if Shelly McMarton is the rightful winner. It's dangerous and irresponsible of Cript to say things like that.*

***

Anna read what was posted on *The Representative* and shook her head. Yeri put his arm around her and asked what she was reading.

While he scanned the same editorial, she said, "I don't like Reginald. I'd never vote for him. He's a dirt bag. But—"

Yeri got to the end and interrupted. "I already know what you're going to say." He added, "It was only a couple months ago that almost every part of the first round of voting was manipulated to benefit McMarton. It's not inconceivable that it would happen again."

"Exactly," she said. "You know what the worst part is? They forced me to agree with something Cript said."

***

Later that day, another post was created on *The Representative*'s website. It said:

*In my previous note to the faculty and students, I mentioned I had concluded my investigation of a particular student's use of the academy email. Due to recent developments, I am updating that assessment.*

*During a different and unconnected inquiry into a student's possible discipline, I learned of the existence of additional emails related to my previous investigation. I am now determining if those new emails might require me to alter my previous recommendation of no punishment being handed down to the student.*

247

It was signed by Jim Comb, Head of Student Security.

*** 

As soon as Reginald Cript heard of Mr. Comb's statement he yelled down the hallway of the academy. "Maybe this election isn't so rigged after all!"

*** 

The few students still remaining in the hallway after the last bell of the day heard something entirely different. Standing outside Mr. Podulski's classroom, the door closed, they heard a girl shrieking with fury and what sounded like the Economics teacher trying his best to calm her down.

# 21

That evening, *The Representative* posted an article saying the Head of Student Security should have waited until after the election for senior class president to make such an announcement. It was irresponsible to say such a thing now. Maybe, they said, Mr. Comb should resign.

*** 

"I don't understand," Anna said after reading what the school paper had posted. "They're arguing in favor of the kids not knowing about this before they make a decision that will impact who leads the academy next year? Wouldn't that be even more irresponsible?"

Yeri took the idea and ran with it. A few minutes later, that concept was conveyed in the latest post to *Notes from the Underground.*

\*\*\*

The next day was a blur. No one knew when Mr. Comb's investigation would be complete. Supporters of Cript wanted to see Shelly punished before the election so she would finally be held accountable for all of her backroom dealings. These were the students who knew there was no way she would be punished after she became senior class president. Supporters of McMarton wanted her cleared before the election so she could win without a shadow hanging over her head.

Regardless of what happened the following day, the Traditionalists swore they would fight from the very first day of the next school year to have Shelly expelled. Reformists were largely quiet, knowing that this was what they had signed up for when they picked her to be their candidate.

\*\*\*

Only hours before the first votes were to be cast, another post was added to *The Representative*'s website.

*I have concluded my investigation of the new emails and have found that the student in question should still be cleared of all charges.*

*Sincerely,*
*Jim Comb*
*Head of Student Security*

\*\*\*

Reginald heard of Mr. Comb's announcement as soon as he arrived to school.

"You've got to be shitting me!" he screamed. "The entire election is rigged!"

# 22

*In only a few minutes, students will begin voting for senior class president. The latest polling shows Shelly McMarton leading in all of the key classrooms that will ultimately decide the election. We at The Representative join the student body in saying we are glad this race will finally be over. This has been the nastiest election we have ever covered, between the two most disliked candidates the academy has ever put forth.*

\*\*\*

Wade Copper, the Statistics teacher, also posted to the academy's website. He said that even after Mr. Comb's brief re-investigation of McMarton's emails, there was still an eighty-five percent likelihood Shelly would defeat Cript and become the next senior class president.

\*\*\*

One after another, students filed through the gymnasium to cast their votes.

"I held my nose and voted for her," Rachel whispered to Melissa. For her role in helping Shelly, Rachel's father kept his word and agreed not to ground her for the additional three weeks he had threatened her with.

When Melissa didn't say anything, only looked to where Chet Booth was being mocked by a pair of seniors, Rachel tugged on her friend's sleeve.

"You voted for her too, right?"

Melissa gave a bitter laugh. "I couldn't bring myself to vote for that liar. My dad paid me to post stuff on the internet. He never said anything about paying extra for me to actually vote for her."

"But that means you voted for Cript."

"We were screwed either way."

Similar conversations were playing out all across the academy.

***

Mr. McHendricks's scratchy voice came over the academy's public address system after lunch. The vice principal sounded as if he were choking on his own tongue as he croaked out the election results.

"It has been a long year," he said. "Thankfully, it's nearly over." He paused, cleared his throat. "In the election for senior class president, Shelly McMarton won forty-eight percent of the votes. Reginald Cript"—the vice principal coughed over and over while the students of United Exceptionalism waited to hear the news that wouldn't be good, no matter what he said next—"Reginald won forty-seven percent of the votes... But while McMarton got more total votes, Cript won more classrooms—twenty-nine to twenty-one—so he will be the next senior class president."

***

Anna and Yeri stared at each other. Neither of them could believe Cript had actually won. Only after Mr. McHendricks's announcement did they both realize that as much as they had disliked both candidates, they had never seriously thought Shelly would lose, not with the faculty, *The Representative*, and the influential parents all supporting her.

Yeri cringed and said, "I feel sick to my stomach that Cript won... while also feeling overwhelmingly relieved that Shelly didn't. I don't think I've ever felt both emotions at the same time. The funny thing is I would have felt the exact same way if McMarton had won and Reginald had lost."

The rest of the day, everywhere the couple went the vast majority of students offered the same assessment. There were a few die-hard McMarton supporters who cried because they thought Shelly would have given them special favors the following year, and there were a few Cript supporters who thought United Exceptionalism would suddenly transform into a different academy. Everyone else said they weren't happy Reginald had won but they also wouldn't have been happy if Shelly had either. And in that demoralized response was a summation of their year at United Exceptionalism.

Anna and Yeri both tried to make sense of how Cript had actually done it. Maybe it was the very fact that the faculty, *The Representative*, and the alumni all supported Shelly that made so many students reject her. Each of those groups had failed to realize that when they continually made the students pick between the lesser of two evils, the kids might not always choose the correct devil. Or maybe it was the fact that while both candidates were unlikeable, the students picked the unknown doom of Cript's brashness and ego instead of the known calamity that was McMarton's dishonesty and elitism.

\*\*\*

At the end of the day, Reginald asked if he could go on the academy's public address system to make an announcement. Mr. McHendricks thought about reminding the boy that profanity and vulgarity weren't allowed. Seeing that the kid in front of him was going to be leading the academy the following school year, he shrugged and gave Cript the microphone.

"I just wanted to thank everyone who supported me," Reginald began. "And for all those who didn't support me—and there were a lot of you—I'm extending an olive branch and asking for your suggestions. This will be an academy for everyone. I want to find common ground and work toward partnerships, not conflict."

When he was done, he thanked the vice principal for allowing him a chance to speak and then left.

Mr. McHendricks stood there with an open mouth, stunned.

"Why didn't the boy say stuff like that when he was actually running for senior class president?"

***

Mr. Podulski said Shelly wasn't done serving United Exceptionalism. A message was posted to her Facebook page that thanked her supporters. Few people actually saw McMarton with their own eyes, however.

As with all things, some students forgot about her and others continued to resent her. The same amount of kids were disgusted that Cript would be their next senior class president. Most, however, didn't care one way or the other about her or Cript. They just wanted to hang out with their friends, enjoy the rest of their time at United Exceptionalism, and go to college.

***

"What do you want to do?" Anna said, her head resting on her forearm, her body at the edge of her bed.

Yeri looked up at her from the floor where he was

reading *The Representative's* latest discussion board. Without Rachel and Melissa and their army of fake accounts, the chat room was much more truthful, filled with students just like he and Anna, kids who didn't know what to expect.

"I don't know. We could switch schools, but it's only one more year. Even if Cript is a disaster, the year will fly by and it'll be time for us to graduate."

The couple had discussed the exact same scenario countless times, regardless of whether it was Cript or McMarton who had won. Now that a new senior class president had been picked, however, neither of them wanted to commit to deciding on their future.

"I just want to be where you are," she said.

"Same here. If you're at United Exceptionalism, that's where I'll go. If you want to switch schools, I'll do that too."

"It's only for one year."

"Yeah."

"And like you said, the year will be over before we know it."

"Yeah, hopefully."

# EPILOGUE

The summer went by faster than any of the kids wanted it to. Before they knew it another school year had started at the United Exceptionalism Academy for Boys and Girls.

***

Cript immediately set about undoing many of the things the previous senior class president had enacted. This delighted the Traditionalists and dismayed the Reformists. It also ensured that United Exceptionalism, after all the fighting and bickering, was roughly the same institution it had been two years earlier. For all of their talk about the changes both sides wanted, neither seemed to realize that the constant back and forth ensured the academy would never transform into what either wanted. Meanwhile, one of the drinking fountains was still making students sick and nothing was done to fix it.

Only a month into classes and already the football team was sent to settle an argument with another school. They did this the old fashioned way. The senior class president stated that the fighting wasn't something he wished would happen but was necessary for protecting all of the other students.

***

The academy was, the alumni agreed, the greatest school anyone could hope to attend. However, it no longer ranked first in quality of education. That honor went to a private school that was distributing new laptops to all of its students. United Exceptionalism ranked seventh, and the first indications were that in the following year's ranking it might not even be in the top ten. It also no longer ranked first in resources for its students. Kids in some classrooms got headaches from old building materials that had never been updated. Electrical power to some classrooms went out a couple times each year. The road leading into the academy was cracked and worn.

***

The Traditionalist alumni agreed the institution had only gotten to where it was because of previous Reformist senior class presidents. The Reformist alumni agreed the academy had only gotten to this point because of prior Traditionalist senior class presidents. The students just wanted to learn and expand their horizons but this was tough when money for field trips was diverted to pay for lawyers to defend the football team. Much of the budget for school dances was used to settle a lawsuit with an alumnus whose contracting company had only gotten work after donating money to a certain charity.

Although it had more faults than anyone liked to admit, no one could say United Exceptionalism didn't prepare its students for the real world.

# ACKNOWLEGDMENTS

As always, I am indebted to many people for their support. Jodie McFadden's constant encouragement is what keeps me optimistic. My editor, D.L. Mackenzie, can always be trusted to not only fix all of my typos and run-on sentences but also talk through plot points and the key elements of writing. Matt Butterweck, who was one of my earliest readers, can always be counted on for his eagle eye and ideas. Of course, my parents and brother also deserve enormous thanks for their support. I am also grateful to everyone who has ever picked up one of my books, taken some time out of their lives to read it, and then recommend it to their friends. Without their support, I would be nowhere.

Want to receive updates on my future books? Sign up for my newsletter at:  http://chrisdietzel.com/mailing_list/

# ABOUT THE AUTHOR

Chris graduated from Western Maryland College (McDaniel College). He currently lives in Florida. His dream is to write the same kind of stories that have inspired him over the years.

His others novels have been featured on the *Authors on the Air* radio network, been required reading at the university level, and become best-sellers.

www.ingramcontent.com/pod-product-compliance
Lightning Source LLC
Chambersburg PA
CBHW050019180626
46810CB00002B/483